I0788438

THE SUMMER EVERYTHING CHANGED

KARY JANE HUTTO

CONTENTS

*This book is dedicated to, first and foremost,
my son Jacob Hutto. It is for him that I originally wrote this book.
It is also dedicated to my beautiful sister, Sarah, and her son, my nephew,
who was diagnosed at 16. And to my friend's son, who was diagnosed at age
8, and to my other friend whose daughter was diagnosed at age 13.
There are not enough words to express how brave and courageous all of the
children and grown T1D's living daily with type one diabetes are for being
warriors - I revere you living daily with a disease you never asked for!*

*I want to thank my husband, my children and their families, my parents,
siblings, their families, and my friends, who have all supported and
encouraged me over the years!*

*Thanks to my fabulous publisher, Rogue Wolf Publishing, LLC, and my
editor!*

1

SUN. Blue skies. Poolside. Another perfect Texas summer day. This is her happy place. This is her refuge. Her dark hair drapes over the back of the blue and white lounge chair. The sweet smell of pina colada wafts into her nostrils, tantalizing her senses. The sun's rays beat down on her already bronzed skin. Samantha peeks out from under her sunnies to the semi-bronzed, pretty girl lying on the other blue and white lounge chair. Jules, better known as Samantha's best friend in the world, has been in her life since she moved to Texas.

Samantha giggles to herself, and she can practically see her reflection in Jules's skin. It's glistening just about as much as Samantha's since they'd just slathered on more deep-tanning oil. Samantha turns, lies back, pulls her sunnies down, and closes her eyes. A slight breeze floats over their warm bodies, cooling them ever so slightly.

Samantha, as everyone calls her, thinks *this summer will be just as great as the last four have been! Nothing can ruin it, especially with Jules by my side!*

"Mmm," she tells Jules, "I love the smell of suntan oil."

"Me too!" Jules agrees happily. "Me, too!"

It does seem to Samantha that the days seem to pass quicker each summer.

Why does it feel like this as we get older?

The girls have just under two months before their ninth grade year starts, and they are determined to relax as much as possible, before "reality" hits. Samantha's thoughts take her back to four years ago, when, at a mutual friend's birthday party, she and Jules met. Six months ago, Samantha had moved from Utah to Dallas, Texas, and had made a few friends, but no one she'd consider a "bestie."

During some silly game, one of the guys opened a pop can that exploded all over Samantha—her hair, her clothes, the floor—everything! Jules rushed over to help her, slid on the soda, and landed on her bottom, and from that, she became covered in soda, too. They both started laughing hysterically and from that point on, they bonded.

They'd become inseparable friends! Jules and Samantha happen to both be tall with slender builds, making trading clothes very easy. They are opposites in their coloring though. Jules's Norwegian heritage is shown through her white-blond hair, blue eyes, and pale skin, compared to Samantha's Italian heritage—long, dark brown hair, dark features, olive skin, and hazel eyes.

Despite their opposite looks, they are very similar in that they are bright, dedicated students, plus they are also in the school choir together. When they aren't hanging together, they are talking or texting on their cells. Everyone knows that Samantha and Jules are inseparable and are best friends, and that *nothing* can tear them apart. Nada!

Suddenly, Samantha's memories are interrupted as she feels cold water all over her. She abruptly sits up and sees her older brother Rocco burst through the water's surface, laughing as he yells, "Got ya!"

"Thanks so much, buddy," she growls through her fake smile and semi-clenched teeth. Oh! How Rocco loves to tease and annoy her anytime and anywhere! He continues to splash around as they receive another splash of water. As they are drying off, they both get splashed AGAIN.

"Rocco! Pleaseeeee!" Samantha screams, and she turns to seriously ball Rocco out as a tall, dark-haired, and very tanned rando boy breaks the surface of the water.

"Oh! I'm so sorry, I, um, well… ha, I didn't mean to yell at you. That was meant for my stupid brother." Samantha is glaring at Rocco now sending *I'm going to murder you later look* with her eyes.

"Brother? Brah, I've been to your house like ten times this summer and I didn't know you had another sister. Just Janey."

"Sorry, brah. It never came up. Plus, Samantha and Jules live outside, at the mall, or at the movies." Rocco shrugs, and the guy pushes him under the water.

"Well, hi, I'm Bo. And you are?"

Samantha immediately feels her face turn three shades of red, and then she feels Jules grab her arm and sidle beside her.

"Hey, Bo. I'm Jules and this is my bestie, Samantha.

"Hey Bo," Samantha says shyly.

"Nice to meet you both."

And then he's gone under the water as Rocco pops up out of it, and they both start to wrestle with each other and splash more water out of the pool. The girls grab their now-soaked towels and lotions and such and walk to where the dry towels are kept.

"Okay, now, he's hot! Maybe not as hot as your brother, but still hot!" Jules excitedly says.

"Woah. Rewind. My brother is *not* hot. He's annoying, but Bo **is** really hot. He's so good looking, and I probably sounded like a blubbering idiot."

"Ha! You have a very adorable, annoying brother. And you did not." Jules laughs. "Well, not too much anyway! And when did Rocco get so tall and so good-looking?"

"Rocco is not good-looking! He's an actual knucklehead."

"Well, he's a very cute knucklehead," Jules argues. "And wow, he's so tan and well… hot."

"Ew. Okay, you can never say that again! I may hurl!"

They look at each other and start to laugh hysterically.

"Come on. You need to be ready for your mom, who I bet you five bucks will honk twice when she arrives!"

"For real," Jules agrees. "I tell her every time. Mom! Just text HERE and I'll come out!"

They continue to laugh as Samantha opens the French doors and ushers in Jules. They sprint upstairs to change, and Jules packs her drawstring bag with Samantha's now sopping-wet suit and towel.

"Ugh. We're so wet. Rocco is such an idiot!" Samantha complains.

"But a very hot idiot with his very hot friend!"

They explode into girlie giggles again. As Jules changes and stuffs her wet stuff into her bag, they descend the stairs and go into Samantha's front room to wait for Jules's mom.

"Bo is really cute, isn't he!"

"Freaking cute. Not my type, but you two literally match! Dark skin and dark hair!"

"Yeah, and he seems as tall as Rocco, maybe taller." Samantha has a dreamy look on her face. Then they hear it: two honks as Jules's mom's van comes into sight. They laugh hysterically.

"You owe me five bucks," Samantha calls out to Jules as she walks to her van. She turns and waves goodbye. See you tomorrow!"

"For sure. Thanks for a great day. I'll text ya later on." Samantha gives one more wave and giggles as she shuts the front door. They both love Jules's mom. She's great!

It's always been easy for Jules to be friends with Samantha. Since the day at that silly birthday party five years ago when the soda exploded all over her, they have literally been inseparable. It's what keeps Jules sane in her crazy life. She's the oldest of five kids. She's the oldest, then her brother Jeff (eleven), her sister Elizabeth (nine), then Heather (five), and her youngest brother, Miles—he's two… cute, but wild, ha, ha!

So, she's got a lot going on at home and all around her all the time. She doesn't mind being the oldest, but sometimes she definitely wishes she was an only child. This is why Samantha keeps Jules sane. There are just three kids in Samantha's family, and

Samantha and Rocco are like a year apart, so any time Jules hangs over at Samantha's house, it's not as nuts as her crazy home front. Which is cool for her.

Samantha sometimes comes to Jules's house, but they usually hang out at Samantha's. Plus, she has a pool, so duh, it's already better than her house. When they aren't hanging together, they're talking or texting each other on their cells. Everyone knows she and Samantha are inseparable best friends. Nothing could ever tear them apart!

After Jules leaves, Samantha heads toward the kitchen. Their house has a long front entryway into the kitchen and family room. She decides it's best to go and help her mom make dinner. As Samantha is about to turn the corner while putting on her cute pink ruffled swim cover, a sudden pang aches in her stomach that almost doubles her over.

"Ummmm, ow! What the… I must be hungry, maybe?" she whispers to herself as she heads over to the very long kitchen island to ask her mom what she can do to help with dinner prep. She's mulling over her thoughts about this weird stomach as she walks around to the fridge and stops.

Have I been feeling like I've had a stomachache before dinnertime multiple times this past week? I think so. Maybe it's just something I've been eating? Like, a touch of the stomach flu? I don't know. I'm a growing girl, right? My appetite is just increasing. Yeah, that's got to be it!

"Samantha, you good?" her mom asks her.

Samantha immediately stands erect and snaps out of her reverie quickly. "Yeah, yeah, of course, ha… just thinking about a movie choice for us to watch later tonight if you're available." Samantha grins as she says this.

"Oh, great idea! Dad and Rocco are going to a movie later, and Janey is at Claire's house, so yes, let's do it!"

Phew! Glad that worked.

Samantha continues to ask questions to distract her mom from asking her any more questions.

"Claire? Who's that?"

"Oh, you know that nice boy Bo who's been hanging here with Rocco? Well, it's his little sister, and she and Janey met at the park a few weeks ago and now they're fast friends."

"Cool. Yeah, Jules and I met Bo today after both he and Rocco splashed us and we got soaked!"

"Honestly! Rocco!" Mom says exasperatedly.

"Yeah… agreed! So, um, did they move here recently, or what?"

"I believe so. I think this past March, from Illinois, maybe. I'm not entirely sure. I need to talk with his mom again."

Mom turns back around and faces the fridge again. Then, she pulls the ingredients needed to make dinner from the fridge and puts them all on the countertop.

Okay, stomach. Let's just settle down now. I don't want to make a big deal out of something that I know isn't even a big deal.

"Hey sweetie, could you dice the tomatoes and shred the lettuce, please? Oh, and fill two bows with the Mexi-cheese, too."

"Sure thing. That's why I'm here! To help you fix dinner," Samantha answers cheerfully.

"I appreciate that. Thank you."

I wash the tomatoes and lettuce, chop and shred them to distract myself from my weird musings, and then empty the already-grated cheese into two bowls.

"Must be taco salad night!" I declare happily.

"You got it!" Mom answers cheerfully, and she gives me such a beautiful and warm smile. I am one lucky girl to have the mother I have. She's just a peach.

2

DINNERTIME IS ALWAYS a good time for Samantha. They talk. They laugh. They visit. They eat. It's been a family tradition for as long as she can remember, and she sure hopes they can keep it up for years to come even as they get older! Dish duty falls to her dad and Rocco tonight. Rocco tries to disappear by muttering about some sort of video game tournament or something or other, and he jogs up the stairs so quickly!

"Nice try, buddy," her dad says to Rocco, calling him up the stairs. "Get your body downstairs immediately!" He's laughing as he says this though.

Samantha hears a huge sigh and hands being dragged on the walls of the stairwell.

"Rocco!" Samantha mutters to herself and rolls her eyes for the second time today over his antics. She has put up all the leftovers and saunters into the TV room and sees her mom sitting outside sipping her water bottle. She grabs hers too, fills it up, and walks out to join her.

Texas *never* cools down in the summer, even at night, so if you like the heat, then Texas is the place for you.

"Don't you just love our backyard!" She sighs, slides into a chair beside her mom, and sits down. She loves to just gaze at the beautiful bougainvillea and the magnolia trees.

Her mom nods her head and the sit there for a good while before the mosquitoes start their evening attack.

I love living in Texas! Except for the blasted bugs ha, ha.

"Time to go inside!" they both say simultaneously!

Since the kitchen is all clean, and it is still early, Samantha excuses herself and asks her mom if they can watch their movie in about an hour.

"I'm going to chill in my room for a bit. Text me when you're ready, will ya?"

"Sure thing, sweetie," her mom says as she pulls out the book she's been reading this week.

Samantha takes her time as she walks upstairs. Rocco's room is the first room on the right, just off the stairs. Samantha's is in the second room on the right, and Janey's room is on the left. Their parents' room is on the first floor. She grabs her phone and puts on her "faves" playlist on Apple Music. As Samantha's swiping through Instagram, she suddenly clutches her stomach.

"Ohhh, owww! Not again with this pain. Why am I having these stomach pains?

Am I still hungry?" Samantha is talking aloud to herself again. And then her stomach growls so loudly as if on cue to confirm what she's feeling.

"Weird. Maybe I'll grab a snack in a little bit. But, for real, how can I be hungry? I ate all of Mom's dinner. I mean it was taco salad—one of my favorites—and I even had two servings!"

She tries to ignore the gnawing hunger pains and continues to scroll.

PING.

It's Jules.

Jules: *"Gurll what's up?"*

Samantha: *"Just finished dinner chillin till I watch a movie with my mom. U?"*

Jules: *"Yeah just chillin too listening to music. Need to clean my gross* *room"*

Samantha: *"OMG me too. Mine is awful. Should we go to a movie tomorrow then swim?"*

Jules: *"For sure"*

Samantha: *"Maybe we should ask Rocco and Bo to join us?"*

Jules: *"Maybe? I can ask Rocco. G'night!"*

Samantha: *"G'night back. Txt when ur up"*

Samantha pushes play on her phone to continue playing her music again.

I can never, ever, ever survive doing anything without music.

She flings her phone onto her very unmade bed, surveys her clothes-covered floor, and begins the task of cleaning up her room. Her mom has been nagging her all week to clean her room, so tonight is just as good as any other time to start.

Her room is finally clean between texts and changing songs a million times. She has the largest pile of laundry to wash and fifty things to hang up, too, but her stomach is killing her too badly, and she can no longer handle her hunger.

Perfect timing as she has just started walking down the stairs and gets a text from her mom to "come on downstairs," to watch their movie—*Princess Diaries*. She loves that movie! But first, she veers into the kitchen to get some cookies and milk. She flips through the latest National Geographic her dad has left on the countertop while she eats a handful of cookies and drinks a glass of milk. Samantha ends up drinking two glasses of milk and eating six cookies!

Finally, she is feeling a bit better and no longer feels starving, so she can now go into the TV room. She promptly plops down onto the couch by her mom.

"Hey Ma."

"Hey darlin', ready to watch our show?"

"You bet!" Samantha smiles and queues it up on one of their streaming platforms.

They both settle back, chat and watch the entire movie. Oh, how Samantha just loves hanging out with her mom—probs not common for some teens—but she and her mom, and Janey, for that matter, love to be together and do lots of girly things together.

* * *

MEANWHILE, JULES SLEPT SOMEWHAT FITFULLY, SO SHE ENDS UP sleeping in until 10:00 A.M.! Dang. She quickly gets dressed and texts Samantha.

Jules: *"Sorry, Sam. Slept crappy so I slept in."*

Samantha doesn't answer immediately, so she heads to the kitchen to rustle up something for breakfast.

Finally, Samantha answers.

Samantha: *"Don't feel bad. I've only been awake for a little bit anyway"*

Jules: *"I'm gonna eat and head over to your house. Is that cool?"*

Samantha: *"Sure, sure. See you in a bit"*

Jules packs her backpack with a towel, suit, suit cover, water bottle, wallet, phone charger, and a change of clothes for the day.

I never know what we will end up doing when Samantha and I hang out, so it's better to be prepared. Rocco will surely be around, and I always want to look cute! She smiles to herself as she finishes packing up her stuff.

"Mom! Mom???"

She hears her mom from the other room. "In with Miles! Why are you yelling?"

"Mom! I need a ride to Samantha's house. Like now!"

"Is your room clean?"

"Yes, it is! I cleaned it last night."

"Is the dishwasher emptied?"

CRAP!

"No! If I do that THEN can you drop me off?"

"Yes, yes."

"Sweet. Thanks!"

* * *

SAMANTHA IS HANGING UP HER CLOTHES WHEN THE DOORBELL RINGS.

Must be Jules!

She takes the stairs two at a time and walks quickly to her front door. "Well, good morning sunshine!"

"Hey, Samantha! Sorry, I'm late. Had to empty the dishwasher."

"All good. Come on up to my room with me. Trying to hang up all of the clothes I found after digging through the piles on my floor!"

"Ugh. I did the same thing last night! I'll help ya."

They chatter like happy squirrels finding nuts as they head up the stairs into Samantha's room. As they pass Rocco's room, they see that both boys are already gaming, but they look up as the girls pass by. Bo smiles as he considers Samantha and Rocco definitely smiles at Jules.

Bo is so freaking cute! But he and Rocco are a year older than Jules and me, and I'm sure he'd want nothing to do with a lowly sophomore in high school. Sigh. One can dream.

Jules and Samantha give the boys their best smiles and wave as they walk to Samantha's room.

"OH MY GOSH. Your brother is so hot!"

"K. Let's be clear. I cannot unhear that now, so thanks!" The girls bust up laughing.

"But how hot is Bo?" Samantha feels her cheeks turn pink as she says this.

"You guys are totally matchy, too! His dark hair and dark eyes are just like yours! But Rocco and I are complete opposites. He's so dark and tan and dreamy…."

"And with that comment, let's get to work, ha, ha!"

They laugh and continue to discuss Bo and Rocco as they fall into a rhythm where Jules hands Samantha an item to be hung up and Samantha hangs it up in her closet. She has it pretty organized—shirts on the left, and skirts and pants below, dresses on the right side. Samantha loves clothes, like a lot. And she has a lot of clothes and knows also this is why Jules likes to borrow her clothes, which is totally cool with her because she has a lot to share!

Jules has so many siblings, so you know money is tight. She's not poor, but you know she's not rich. Anyway, it doesn't matter because I'm glad to share.

* * *

ROCCO IS KILLING THEIR OPPONENTS WHEN HE GETS DISTRACTED AND wanders off into thought. *So yeah, maybe I think Samantha's best friend, Jules, is <u>beautiful</u>. She is a year younger than me. Is that cool? I don't know. Who knows if anything could happen? Would it be weird because she's here all the time and like Samantha's bestie? I just don't know....*

"Dude! Wake up!"

"Sorry, sorry!"

"Where is your brain at right now?"

Rocco just grins sheepishly.

"Okay, I get it," Bo says. "Me too. We need to talk about this later on. Let's finish this part of the game and take a break."

The boys wrap up their game and head to the kitchen—snack time. As they sit around the large countertop dipping cookies into huge glasses of milk (Bo uses a fork and puts it in between the cookie layers—no soggy milk fingers), the girls walk through the back double French doors from the outdoor patio and pool area.

"Oh my gosh! Do YOU use a fork too? SO DO I!" Samantha laughs as she says this to Bo.

"Only way to eat this kind of delish cookie in milk!"

Both girls grab large glasses of milk too and stacks of cookies. They're all eating and laughing when Janey and Claire come running through the kitchen chasing the dog, Daisy Doodle.

Their mom is following them. "Janey and Claire, outside please with Daisy Doodle!" She stops abruptly as she sees all four teens gulping huge glasses of milk and munching on their fave cookies. "Oh, my! Y'all must be hungry! I can make some popcorn or some sandwiches."

"Oh, no, no, don't even worry about that Mrs. Hansen. We're good." Bo smiles and his teeth are covered in black.

They all crack up! Samantha almost spits her milk out!

They finish their milk and cookies, clean up their messes, and decide to go hang out by the pool until Jules's mom comes to get her.

Samantha jumps up quickly at the double honks to escort Jules out through the side gate—not to be polite, but to hide the fact that her stomach is hurting… again. Samantha waves and stands on the grass for a little bit until her stomach cramps subside and she can then walk back to the backyard.

Bo and Rocco are hanging out on the blue and white lounge chairs, so she pulls another chair over to sit by them.

3

"So, Samantha, what classes did you sign up for this year?" Bo asks.

"Year two basics: math, science, history, and ELAR, Spanish three, plus art and beginning pickleball."

"Stellar schedule. I play pickleball. We should play once you learn how to play."

"Deal."

He starts to stand up. "Well, I gotta go. Watching Claire tonight while my parents go out."

"That's so sweet of you!"

"Well, Claire is a good little sister-thankfully-so it's not a big deal."

"Still, I'm sure your parents appreciate it," Samantha says. "And I'm sure you'd rather be doing something else, right?"

"I mean sure, but it's only every so often so I don't mind. See y'all' later."

"Bye, Bo," Rocco and Samantha say in sync.

They hear Bo call for Claire to go home. Samantha stays seated and Rocco leans back and closes his eyes.

"Bo is a really nice guy. How the heck did he become friends with you?" Samantha is smiling as she says this.

"Very funny. But he is, isn't he?"

"He is."

"As is Jules. We are lucky to have such awesome friends. I'm trying to get Bo hired on at the country club pool as a lifeguard like me. I start back to work next week. He's basically hired. My boss is just waiting on a few more documents from his old job."

"Is he trained as a lifeguard?"

"Yeah. I guess he was one at his indoor community pool all last year, so works out well."

"It totally does."

"Soooo, I'm just gonna say this," he says. "Jules is hot. Like I don't know when that happened but boy, she's grown up a lot."

"Oh, gross. She said the same thing about you!"

"What? Why didn't you tell me?"

"Cause it's gross!"

"Tell me the deets, and I'll tell you what Bo is saying about you!"

"Woah. Woah, what? He's talking about me to you? Not good ha, ha."

"Ha, ha, very funny. But it's true. He's diggin' you big time."

Samantha squeals and stands up! "He's sooooo cute! I can't!"

"Woah, gross!"

Samantha punches Rocco hard in the shoulder.

"Ow, knock it off! That hurts," Rocco whines while chuckling.

"Baby! Now tell me, please!"

"Okay, okay. Ugh, can't believe I have to say these words out loud, but he thinks you're hot."

"Oh, my gosh, for real?"

"Yes! And it's gross."

"Now you know how I felt as Jules talked nonstop about you today. It's so EW!"

"Luckily dudes don't talk as much as you girls, but I still hear comments here and there so I am painfully aware!"

Samantha punches Rocco again in his arm!

"Dang girl!" he complains. "Relax. Let's go inside. I can't handle this convo anymore."

"Me, neither. I can't even think of you and Jules like together as a couple—so ew!"

"Uh, ditto with you and Bo! Gross."

Rocco and Samantha clean the pool area first before going inside for the day. Rocco closes the pool cover while Samantha folds towels and hangs out the wet ones. Then they both head inside.

They see Janey helping their mom wash the grapes in the sink. Their dad will be home in about an hour, so Rocco and Samantha join Mom and Janey in helping out. With Rocco starting work next week, they all want to take advantage of the time they spend together, especially for dinner. Usually, their friends go home by dinnertime so the Hansen family can be together.

"Hey. should we play Rummikub* tonight?" Samantha asks cheerfully.

"Yay! Let's play," Janey shouts.

"Sure, sure." Mom agrees. "How about cleaning up after dinner?"

Everyone nods in agreement.

* * *

Bo thinks Rocco is cool. He and Bo have known each other since spring after Bo and his family moved from the Chicago area to the Dallas area for his dad's work. The boys both ended up playing on the high school soccer team and also had multiple classes together. And now since Bo met Samantha today, she's literally all he can think of!

A good friend to hang with and his hottie sister? Pffff. Too good to be true!

* * *

Ever since Jules basically "noticed" Rocco a few weeks ago, she can't shut up about him! Okay. To be fair, Samantha has been the very same way with the subject of Bo—s since she met him, and how he's so hot—and luckily for Samantha and Jules, Bo and Rocco have been hanging out every day since they met up in the pool when the boys splashed them.

It's been a little awkward between the four of them cause they're trying to get to know one another better. They run into each other in the kitchen or by the pool all the time now. There's some convo back and forth between them all, but it's still a little hesitant.

From Rocco's point of view, Jules may have always been around, but she was always just Jules—Samantha's bestie—until she wasn't just that for Rocco anymore. Not sure when Jules got all grown up, but she did, and Rocco noticed. And vice versa.

Today is Friday, and they are all by the pool chatting about this and that when an idea pops into Bo's head.

"So, what if we all head to the mall and catch a movie this afternoon?"

"Uh, yeah, I'm in," Samantha said happily, trying to not sound too enthusiastic.

"Yeah, sounds cool," Jules chimes in.

"Okay, it's a plan then," Rocco adds.

"How about we eat lunch here?" Bo suggests. "I'll check the movies, and we can pick one and go."

"Sure"

"Okay"

"Awesome."

Bo smiles as he grabs his phone and opens his Cinemark app. He shouts out a few ideas, and they decide on a new suspense flick for this afternoon at 3:00 P.M.

"Hey, Jules, make me a sandwich, will you? I need to run upstairs really quickly!" Samantha asks as she hurries up the stairs.

"Yeah, of course."

Jules joins the boys, who are already making PB&Js with chips. Samantha clutches her stomach as she goes up the stairs, hoping no one can see her. She runs into her room and rolls herself onto the floor in a ball.

Oh, my gosh, this is insane. Owww. Dang. It hurts. Like cramps. But, I guess, at least the pain ebbs and flows throughout the day, but I never know when! I hope this just goes away!

Samantha's stomach settles down, so she picks up her purse from her nightstand and changes her shoes. She then does a quick check of herself in her stand-alone mirror.

Not too bad!

She smiles at herself and heads downstairs. She rapidly eats her lunch, praying her stomach stays settled. Thankfully, she does feel a bit better after she eats her lunch.

* * *

"K, y'all grab what you need to go to the movies," Rocco tells the girls. "Bo paid for all of us, so here's his Venmo QR code."

Everyone scans the code and sends money to Bo. Rocco grabs his keys and heads towards the front door, where his Honda is parked on the curb. His mind suddenly jumps to where everyone might sit, especially Jules, at the theater. He starts the car and watches as the girls and Bo trickle out the front door. Samantha and Jules both open the back doors and climb into the back seats. Bo awkwardly stands to the side because he was going to open the door for at least Samantha, but they were both already in and buckled. He smiles as Samantha looks up at him from the backseat, then gets himself in and buckles in on the passenger seat.

Rocco gets the music started and they chat happily driving to the mall where their fave theater is located. They live about twenty minutes from Horton Plaza. It's a fabulous mall with outside and inside stores and activities, and the theater is on the bottom floor. Rocco and Bo drop the girls at the curb and park the Honda.

"Dude. How should we sit in the theater?" Bo asks.

"Just what I was thinking of the whole time I was driving us!"

"Okay, what about this: I'll sit by you, you sit by your sister and she sits by Jules? Then it's not weird and awkward. Plus, we've all just begun to hang out. Right?"

"For real, we don't want any awkwardness. K. It's a plan. Sounds good."

Rocco and Bo grab a large popcorn to share and two drinks so the boys and girls can share. Samantha and Jules are already inside the theater and sitting in their seats.

* * *

"Woah. Who's going to sit by whom?" Samantha asks.

"Blast! I didn't even think about that, Samantha!"

"Okay, let's make this easy. I'll just sit by my brother on his left side, and then you sit on my side because we're not at the point where we're all going to sit by who we like. Right?"

"Okay, yeah, that works," Jules agrees. "That's a good idea because I would still feel very awkward sitting by Rocco because you know we're just like noticing each other, and we're in the I've-seen-you're-hot stage!"

"Okay, ew, I don't know if I'm going to be able to get used to you thinking my brother Rocco, who is a knucklehead is hot. But I'm trying to adjust to the whole idea. Anyway, yes, I agree."

They both settle into their chairs and see the boys coming their way. Samantha had texted Rocco right after her convo with Jules to say that he sits by her, Bo can sit to his left, and Jules can sit to her right. He agreed with that and said that he and Bo had had the very same type of convo, so there would be no awkwardness.

The girls watch as the two boys come toward the girls to sit down.

$$4$$

THE MOVIE IS AWESOME, and the foursome had a great time together sharing the popcorn, laughing, and getting freaked out at the movie altogether. Luckily, Samantha's stomach wasn't cramping. For which she was so grateful. And she was able to eat the popcorn and drink the soda pop.

As they were nearing the house, Rocco asked if Jules needed to be dropped off.

"Yes, please Rocco. I appreciate that. Then my mom won't have to bring her van with twenty kids and honk for me!"

They all laugh again because it is true without fail: her mom honks whenever she comes to get Jules. It's a really funny habit, but moms will be moms, and you just kind of roll with it sometimes. Bo has his Kia at their house, and since it is after their normal dinner time, Bo waves goodbye to Rocco and Samantha and hops in his car to head home. Rocco parks, and a very good discussion breaks out between the siblings.

"So, thanks for texting me. Bo and I had already stressed about that before the whole movie, so I'm glad that you said that so it wasn't awkward for all of us."

"Yeah, me too. Jules and I were talking about it in the theater while you guys were getting the soda pops and popcorn, and I realized—dude, I gotta text you right now so it's not awkward when you and Bo walk into the theater to find us and find our seats. But it worked out well. We had a good time, so maybe this is something we can all do together here and there?"

"I'm feeling it. Yeah. I think that will be a good thing for us this summer. I was worried—I'm not gonna lie—because Jules is a year younger than me and I'm even older in my grade, so it was almost like she's a year and a half younger than me. But it's cool now cause you know I've always liked her because she's been your bestie. But it's kind of weird for me to notice that she's actually really cute and super adorable and fun and nice."

"Oh, my. Between you and Jules, I'm gonna hurl with these conversations ha, ha!"

"Ditto! How do you think I feel every time Bo opens his mouth and says your sister is so hot? She's so tan. She's so nice. She's so… blah, blah, blah!"

"Okay, touché! We both have our work cut out for us as we have to try not to gag when our friends talk about us to each other. What a weird situation. I would've never thought that you would've found a friend that I would think is absolutely adorable, tan, hot, amazing, and just hot!"

"And now I'm going to say eww!"

They both laugh as they get out of the car and go to see if they can help their mom prepare dinner. Janey should be there with Claire today. Mom told them she'd be eating with them and hanging out. This is kind of good for Samantha because she can get to know Claire as a gateway to learning more about Bo.

After dinner, Samantha is chilling in her room doing her favorite things: listening to music and sketching. She has her art idea app open and is collecting ideas and drawing some of them. She likes to draw and sketch when she's thinking about things and lately, she's had a lot to think about. Between Bo, Rocco, and Jules, and the stomach cramp stuff, her mind has been full of wayyy too many thoughts!

And then out of the blue, here came the cramps. AGAIN. She curls into a ball, which seems to help the pain subside.

This is getting ridiculous! This pain is too much! Knowing when the pains were coming could help me a lot, but they're so sporadic.

JUNE TURNS OUT TO BE THE BEST MONTH IN SAMANTHA'S YOUNG LIFE. Even better than the last five years with her family and Jules because almost every day, Rocco, Jules, Samantha, and Bo did everything together! It has been beyond fun. Movies. Out to eat. Swimming. Shopping—yeah, even the boys have been shopping!

Bo and Rocco taught the girls how to play video games with them, and that has been way too much fun! Samantha's mom and Jules's mom have been cool with all this, but! They've been very, very clear that they do not hang alone, nor behind closed doors. Samantha is a little worried that Bo will think she and Rocco were the most primitive peeps ever! But apparently, his mom is the same as Jules's and theirs, so yay for this!

July hits with a heat vengeance known only to a few places—Texas, Arizona, and Nevada. The temperatures are now a hundred degrees daily, so it's hot and humid. Samantha loves hot weather, and survival is possible because she and her family have a pool. Thankfully, school shopping happens in Texas, too, in July, even though it won't get even slightly cool until November! So, they can all stay out of the heat in the A/C or the pool.

The boys have had work sporadically and end up having the same shifts, so that's been great for them, Jules, and Samantha to coordinate their social activities with them.

A typical summer day for Samantha, Jules, Rocco, and Bo involves meeting at Samantha and Rocco's house, making a plan for the day, and executing it! Rocco and Bo always work a few days per week, so that's part of their weekly plans. They need to earn money for college, but it's a good job that allows them all to hang out together.

These stomach cramps are killing me. I think they are increasing each week! I will tell my mom in the next week or so if they don't stop.

Samantha continues to find ways to pretend she needs to "do something" if she feels the blasted stomach cramps coming on. So far, so good, but she's not so sure she can keep this up! It's wearing her out. Plus, it's that time of the year to start getting school supplies in the next few weeks because all the stores put out the school supply items in July.

For Samantha and Jules, clothes shopping is a top priority since they love clothes. In fact, Samantha digs dopamine dressing (Samantha found this concept online some time ago), meaning that you dress to make yourself happy. It raises your dopamine levels, which in turn makes you so, so happy! For Samantha, this is the exact definition of how she shops and dresses.

One thing that Samantha and Jules love to do is go thrifting together. It's low-key their favorite thing to do together. It helps Jules's budget, and Samantha loves to mix her fab thrift finds with her other clothing items. For them both, it ends up extending their wardrobe majorly. And you see excellent designer brands for so cheap. And they realize that they're upcycling, too, instead of adding more to the landfills. They have a cute store called "Thrifty Pennies," which they frequent weekly during summer.

Luckily, the school year doesn't start until August 16, giving everyone a few more weeks to prepare for school. Samantha, Jules, Rocco, and Bo have more weeks to hang out, the boys to hang out, and the girls to thrift and shop. The dudes don't care that much. They both dress well, and Rocco will get some new clothes. Rocco told Samantha the other day that he doesn't care as much as Samantha does.

For Samantha and Jules, since they'll be going in as sophomores in high school, they've gotta upgrade their wardrobes and be comfortable at the same time, because, as the girls learned their freshman year in high school, there aren't any lockers and they have to carry around their backpacks all day with all of their books, so in dressing and purchasing items for high school, that's something to consider in their clothing choices.

"Rocco!"

"What, sis?"

"When are you going shopping for clothes for school?"

"Whyyyyy?"

"Cause I need to go with you, please."

"Can we go tomorrow? I've got an early shift."

"That sounds great! Thanks, Rocco!"

"Do you think you two could text like normal teens?" Mom giggles as she mentions this suggestion to her eldest kiddos.

"What fun is that, Mom? Shouting up and down the stairs is so much more fun!" Rocco winks at his mom and runs outside.

"That child! Honestly!"

* * *

THE WEEKS ARE PROGRESSING. JULES AND ROCCO ARE LOOKING PRETTY tight these days. Unfortunately for Samantha, her stomach cramps aren't helping her potential love life one bit! Samantha's stomach cramping has continued to increase and not abate.

THIS IS NOT A GOOD SIGN! Increasing stomach cramps is no bueno. I need them to STOP!

In fact, it is stressing Samantha right out now. She's very concerned as to why it keeps going on and on, but she tends to push it aside because she can work through it or chalk it up to something she may have eaten or that she eats all the time.

But in the back of Samantha's mind, there is one thought that niggles in her brain at some point: she may have to tell her mom if this stomach cramping continues to cause it may be something serious.

Right now, it's the second week of July, and Samantha's sole purpose each day is to enjoy this month fully because she surely knows that August 16th will come sooner rather than later. Samantha is chilling in the TV room waiting for Jules to show up this morning.

They're gonna go thrift while the boys are at work today. Despite the stomach aches and cramping, she can't help but think that her life is in a really good spot.

My life is so good right now, and I love living here in Dallas! I loved living in Utah, and I had a lot of great friends, but Dallas has turned out terrific. I love my high school, my new friends, my house, and my neighbor-hood—everything is awesome! I am so grateful for Jules, too. I mean I even love my brother, Rocco, even though he is a pain at times, and my little sister, Janey, is just the sweetest girl, and my parents are awesome and loving, so I feel super content.

And Bo. She can honestly say she's super grateful to be getting to know him. Not something she would have thought would happen this summer. I mean, as a sophomore, she really hadn't thought of having a boyfriend. But Samantha won't get ahead of herself. She and Bo aren't even at this point yet, and it isn't something she's even allowed herself to think of this summer.

But has she allowed herself to dream of this possibility? Constantly! Samantha and Bo have really had so much fun together. They have much in common and like many of the same types of movies, food, and such. She's had lots of crushes here and there, but she's never actually gone out or dated any one boy. So, this is a whole new situation! And Samantha wants to do this right and not mess anything up. There's been no handholding at all, but slight arm touches or Bo nudging her, and he's taken to hugging her, saying hello and goodbye each time they see each other. Samantha can't help but smell his fresh scent every time he does this, and her stomach is always all aflutter!

Rocco and Samantha will run errands before meeting Jules and Bo at the Cinemark theater later. There is a double feature today, so they do not want to miss it! Jules has some stuff to do with her family today, and Bo is on shift in the morning, so Rocco and Samantha took advantage of spending some quality sibling time together.

"Thank goodness you have your license, Rocco," Samantha says as they get into his used silver Honda Accord.

"True that! Freedom for us!"

They laugh happily, and Samantha pulls up her playlist to start the music as they cruise together. Samantha clutches her stomach rather aggressively.

Oh crap! NOT again? Argh.

"Yo, Samantha, you okay?"

"Uh, yeah, ha, ha. Yeah, just my stomach is a little bubbly. Maybe the sausage from breakfast?"

"Okay, just let me know if I need to get some Tums for you. Or a Sprite."

"Okay, sure, sure. I promise Rocco, I'm fine. It's just a little bubbly." Samantha manages to give Rocco a weak smile. But she knows he's not stupid and is surely concerned for her. Samantha turns to focus on the playlist.

I feel starved! Like I never, ever, ever ate in my whole life! What in the world is going on with me? I may need to eat again.

"Hey, can we get some lunch, Rocco, before heading to the theater?"

"Of course. How's your stomach?"

"It chilled out," she lies. "Just need some food ha, ha."

They pull into Chick-fil-A and grab some nugget meals. She scarfs down her food.

"Dang girl! You were really hungry, ha, ha!"

"I told ya!"

BUT my stomach still feels yucky. Maybe, once the food hits my stomach it'll feel better. But I know that I'm just trying to convince myself, but it's not like there's actually something wrong with me... is there?

It's hard for Samantha to even think that something could be wrong with her because she's been perfectly healthy her whole life. It has to be a gastrointestinal issue—at least, that's what she hopes.

"It's almost halfway through July!" Samantha says to her mom as she enters the kitchen area to get some breakfast.

"It's true. Sometimes I feel like days pass more quickly than they used to," her mom muses aloud.

"I totes agree, sheesh! Why so fast summer, why so fast?" Samantha gets a bowl and pours in some shredded tweets, her fave.

She pours some milk in and starts to munch her cereal.

Immediately after Samantha has finished eating, her stomach growls and begins to hurt.

CRAP. School is literally in five weeks now! And my stomach continues to hurt!! I am glad that Jules and I have spent A LOT of time with Bo and Rocco. Hanging together distracts me from my dumb stomach issues and aches. And I'm not gonna lie. It's been awesome.

5

"Less than five weeks left until school?" Samantha is talking to herself as she puts away all the new clothes she's been buying and is working on sorting her closet. She also cleans through every piece of clothing she no longer wears and always gives Jules the first pick, then the rest she donates.

As she goes through her sock and undies drawer, her mind wanders to yesterday when Jules, Rocco, Bo, and she went to the mall to get some shoes. Bo ended up walking really close to her, and Samantha could feel his arm in her arm. It was tantalizing! It's all she's been able to think of—how close she was to Bo. He always smells fresh and clean, and Samantha sees that she likes Bo more and more.

As she moves on to hanging up her new jeans and shirts, a sudden wave of sickness comes over Samantha, and she legit feels as if she's gonna hurl.

Oh crap. This is getting ridiculous. It's every day, all day long now.

Okay, here's what I'm gonna do: if this keeps up for one more week, I'm telling Mom—final decision.

After finishing putting everything away, Samantha realizes she has two big bags of clothing and other items for Jules to go through. She quickly texts her.

Samantha: *"Cleaned through my clothes. Guess who has two bags to rifle through? U!"*

Jules: *"OMG you're the best Samantha, for real. Thank you. Can I do that when I come over tomorrow?"*

Samantha: *"Sure thing—see ya tomorrow"*

Jules: *"Perf!"*

Now, for the backpack and school supplies! I don't know why I love *school supplies, but I really do!*

Samantha plops down on her floor and begins the ritual of labeling and organizing items per class. She pulls out her class schedule from her wallet.

Geography, English, science, math, lunch, PALS, Spanish and Art. Great schedule, if I say so myself! Plus, Jules and I are in Spanish together.

* * *

July 13

Two days after another back-to-school shopping spree, Samantha wakes up in the middle of the night to go to the bathroom. She doesn't think too much about it that night, but she certainly does the next night, when she wakes up two times to go to the bathroom. In fact, over the whole next few days Samantha feels so thirsty, and so hungry too. She's having to go to the bathroom a lot too both during the day AND now about three times every night!

I'm sort of really concerned. But wait. I am overreacting, as it is still July and so hot. I am obviously drinking more, so I must go to the bathroom more. I am trying to be reasonable and rational, but... I think I may need to tell my mom—and soon.

But by the beginning of the next week, things are not good. Samantha's stomach hurts badly all the time. She is really thirsty, and she goes to the bathroom every couple of hours during the day and at night. PLUS, she is always ravenous! I mean, she's eating and then feels hungry. Samantha hadn't said anything to her parents, siblings, or even Jules, and especially not Bo. She's had to bow out a lot over the last two weeks due to how she's feeling! Ugh. And she's lost weight. The clothes she bought like two weeks ago are loose.

"What is wrong with me?" she says aloud in her bathroom. Samantha doesn't realize she'd even said it aloud until Jules says something.

"What's up, Samantha? Who are you talking to?" Jules asks suspiciously.

"Oh, yeah, ha, ha. No one, silly," Samantha says. "I am just talking to myself."

"Okay, you sure?" Jules says to Samantha.

"Yeah, totally fine."

Lie. Lie. Lie. I am NOT FINE.

* * *

July 15

Even though Samantha has managed to keep her night wakings, excessive thirst, and feeding frenzies to herself—she did have a good appetite fortunately, so eating extra isn't that big of a deal—but this going to the bathroom a lot during the day situation is proving to be a problem. So, Samantha resolves to tell her mom tonight after she and Jules get back from the movies and maybe see if her mom can get her in to see Doc Jopling, their pediatrician, before school starts on Monday.

I'm sure I'm just being overly dramatic. I mean, what could possibly be wrong with me??

Samantha, Rocco, Jules, and Bo are still hanging out, but Samantha decides to hang out with just Jules today. She figures she can cover up any sick issues she may have while hanging with Jules. She was afraid that Bo and Rocco would ask her too many questions if they all ended up at the movies again together.

Samantha ends up having to go to the bathroom three times during their movie, and she gets frustrated.

"This is ridiculous!" she whispers to herself the third time she leaves the theater. Jules even asks her if she is okay, and Samantha can blame the thirty-two-ounce drink she'd purchased with her popcorn. This seems to pacify Jules, but Samantha is now more eager than ever to get home and talk to her mom.

Enough is enough!

Samantha realizes she is actually also feeling super crappy, and so this is really the last straw. The bathroom pit stops have gotten out of control, along with all the other stuff, and now she's missing the freaking movie, ugh!

Jules's mom drops Samantha home after the movie.

"Thanks, Mrs. Barker. Bye, Jules! See ya tomorrow."

"See ya, Samantha!"

Samantha waves, and as soon as Jules is out of sight, she practically sprints to the front door. She opens it with such force that she accidentally slams it shut.

"Mom? Mom?" Samantha calls as she runs into her house.

She really wanted to meet up with Bo and Rocco at the movie but had to make up some lame excuse as to why they couldn't. So dumb, and just as things are getting really good with Bo—not like holding hands or kissing or anything. Just being by him these days made her stomach flutter with lovely butterflies. Same with Jules and Rocco. They're actually really compatible together. Argh. Samantha is so frustrated!

"Mom, where are you?" Samantha is feeling frantic now and tears are welling up in her eyes.

"I'm outside, Sam," her mom's pleasant voice calls back.

She tears open the right-side French door and searches the yard to find her mom. She's tending to her plants. She loves her flowers and loves pruning and preening them, but there's no time for that now.

"Mom, I need to talk to you." Samantha is practically out of breath and is feeling very apprehensive.

"Good gracious. What's going on?"

"Mom, I, I think something's going on with me, um… I'm not feeling really well. I'm thirsty all the time, and my stomach hurts so badly. I've even lost weight! And I'm constantly hungry and my stomach has been cramping up so badly and I have to go to the bathroom all the time." Samantha blurts all of this out very rapidly without even taking a breath, and then the tears come streaming down her face.

As so many tears fall down her pretty tanned cheeks, she feels a huge wave of relief sweeping over her whole body-head to toe as she is giving her mom all of these details. Samantha has kept this all inside for well over two months, and it obviously has been weighing on her soul. Samantha's relief is palpable now.

"Sweetie, what in the world are you talking about? What's going on? Do you want me to call Dr. Jopling? And why didn't you tell me sooner? Poor Girl."

Mom speaks softly to Samantha as she walks over to her and pulls Samantha into a momma bear hug.

"Yeah, I do, please. I'm so frustrated, and I need to get some medicine or something." She's blubbering her words since now she's sobbing.

"Sweetheart, look at me."

Samantha pulls back and looks up into her mom's pretty green eyes, wiping her tears away.

"I'll call first thing in the morning sweetie. It will be okay. Dr. Jopling is the best and has always helped us out over the last four years, right?"

Samantha couldn't answer. She just shook her head. She let her mom pull her back into a hug and hold her for a long while.

* * *

July 17

Fortunately, her mom could get her to see Dr. Jopling two days after her emotional breakdown.

Today is Thursday, July 17, and Dr. Jopling luckily has an open appointment at 4:00 P.M.

Samantha had been up for hours. Between her stomach aching and going to the bathroom so much, she was miserable. "I've got to wait all day long. Dang it," she growls. She curls up on the couch and starts to scroll and think.

Her mom has texted Bo's mom to see if Janey could play with Claire while she took Samantha to her appt. Bo and Rocco were on shift today together, which made it easy for Samantha to not worry about any of them hanging out today. Samantha had told Jules that she and her mom were going to a late lunch and shopping, so she felt she'd covered all of her bases. Also, Samantha and Bo had finally exchanged cell phone numbers just the other day. Since they were always hanging together, there hadn't been a real need to do so before this. Jules and Rocco apparently had done this about a month ago. Personally, Samantha wanted to keep things moving along slowly. She is just going to start high school, so why be in a rush?

Samantha is brought out of her thinking storm that clouds her mind when her mom says something.

"I know, Samantha, I know, and I'm very sorry. I guess I'm just glad at least we got in due to a cancellation. I'm counting this as a huge win. I'm going to go drop Janey off and be back. Okay? Just try and relax the best you can. Did you eat anything today?"

"All I've been doing is eating all day, and hey, I still have to pee, and I feel like I'm losing more and more weight!" Samantha is just letting out all of her emotions now that she has told her mom. She feels better. Hiding all of the stuff going on with her has made her way more distressed than she knew, but she is continuing to feel very relieved.

"How about putting on a movie and resting until we have to go? Samantha nods her head, and her mom grabs her favorite blanket and spreads it over her. She hands her the remote too. Samantha smiles and waves as her mom goes through the garage.

"Janey, let's go, sweetie!"

Janey comes bounding down the stairs and skids into the TV room. "What's wrong with you, Sammie?"

"Oh, nothing, sweetie. Just hanging out until Mom comes back. We're going shopping and eating out today. You have so much fun with Claire, okay?"

"Okay! Bye, Sammie!"

Janey is the only one who calls her Sammie. It's very sweet.

Janey runs to the garage inside the door, flings it open, and slams it. Samantha laughs.

"Ten-year-olds!"

Samantha begins to scroll around on a platform and lands on Bob's Burgers. This show makes her and Rocco laugh so much!

And it will hopefully distract me.

While Samantha is chillin' on the couch, she gets a text from Bo.

Bo: *"Hey, Samantha. What's up with you today?"*

Her stomach flutters. She hopes her stomach will always flutter when Bo texts her.

Samantha: *"My mom and I are shopping and going to a late lunch today. Mom and daughter day."*

LIE.

She hates lying to everyone. But hey, this stuff was personal, and she didn't need everyone worrying about absolutely nothing.

Her mom had talked with her dad last night to give him a heads up about what was happening and told him the situation, too—how she'd been feeling and her symptoms. Her dad will pick up Janey on his way home from work. Samantha is glad her mom told her dad, which she obvi assumed she would. Samantha can't help but worry about what would happen if something were really wrong with her. But she'd rather think that maybe there are some meds she can get to cure her, or maybe this is just still some dumb lingering virus.

Man, I hope it's an easy fix!

3:30 pm

FINALLY, IT'S ALMOST TIME TO GO, SO SAMANTHA CHANGED HER clothes quickly. She and her mom climbed into the Suburban and drove to the doctor's office. Samantha taps her fingernails in the car as they drive along the freeway.

"I'm fine, I'm fine," she thinks repeatedly.

Before she knows it, they are at the doctor's office.

Why am I so nervous? Samantha thinks to herself. *I'm so glad I didn't Google my symptoms, or I would have been totally freaked out!*

Her mom checks Samantha in at the front desk, and they sit for like five minutes then her name is called, and Marie, their favorite nurse, takes them back to a room. She asks Samantha to describe what's been going on.

"Well, it all started about two months ago. First, it was just sporadic stomach cramps. It feels like I'm hungry all the time. It's been driving me crazy! But then I have had to go to the bathroom during the night and now so many times per day. I can't keep up!"

"Okay. Thank you, Samantha. I'm entering all this information into your chart. Dr. Jopling will be in shortly."

It's another ten, long agonizing minutes before Dr. Jopling comes in. "Hello, Hansen family!! Good to see you both today. What brings you ladies in today?"

Samantha begins to recount all of the issues that she's been experiencing over the last few weeks.

"So, as I just told Marie, it's been oh, I think maybe two months ago, I was having sporadic stomach aches. Then, about two weeks ago, I started feeling super hungry right after I'd eaten, and actually all day long. It has been this past week or so though, that I've had to go to the bathroom **all the time**. During the night. Constantly throughout the day, and then with the constant hunger and the stomach aches, it's been really difficult and ridiculous. And now this week all of these symptoms have gotten worse and worse. I feel literally so sick and... oh! I'm pretty sure I've lost weight," Samantha says with much exasperation.

She clamps up quickly though, because she can feel tears start to sting her eyes. Just then, Marie knocks on the door and pokes her head in with the sheet of results on Samantha's urine test. Samantha smiles at her. Marie smiles back, but it seems like it is sort of a sad smile. Dr. Jopling thanks her, takes the sheet, and starts to read it. He then slowly raises his head and looks directly at Samantha.

Oh, nooo.

His face shows grim seriousness yet kindness simultaneously. Samantha's palms start to get sweaty.

"Okay, so the first thing that comes to my mind is that we need to check your blood sugar. We will use a blood glucose monitor. Prick a finger. Take some of your blood and check it to see if it represents the measured level of a specific substance in your blood, which will then compare to the normal range for what a typical blood sugar should fall under. I have some suspicions as to what's going on in your body."

Samantha swallows hard before speaking.

"Sure, yeah, I mean we need to figure this out, amiright?" Samantha laughs as she says this.

Dr. Jopling pushed the button to call Marie back into the office. She pops her head into the room.

"Marie, I'd like to check Samantha's blood sugar levels. Would you be willing to get the monitor, test strips, etc.?"

"Sure thing Doc. I'll be right back."

Thankfully, it took her all of about a minute because Samantha was starting to feel tense.

"Okay, darlin', let me see your middle finger, either hand." Samantha puts out her left hand.

"This device has a little lancet, which is basically like the tip of a needle, I crank it and push a button, and it will prick your finger and blood will come out. Then, I will suck up the blood into this test strip, and in about two minutes we will get a number."

Samantha had zero time to process that because Marie did it so quickly. After the two-minute countdown, they patiently waited for the machine to beep.

"690!" Marie practically shouts. They all jump!

"Ah, yes, it is as I suspected, Samantha. Your brain has been thinking the body is starving, and that's why you've been so excessively hungry and thirsty and having frequent urination, as it's called. Your body has actually been fighting against itself. It's called autoimmune, and in this case, your body thinks the cells that produce insulin are the enemy and they are shutting down."

"Okay, say what now?" Samantha asks Dr. Jopling.

"All of this means you have a chronic disease called diabetes mellitus, or T1D, Type 1 diabetes. It means you will have to give yourself insulin anytime you eat anything with carbohydrates in it."

His voice seems to trail off into the distance, and Samantha feels limp. She feels as if she's looking down at herself sitting on the chair next to her mom.

"Samantha? Samantha??" Her mom turns toward her and says something, but even though Samantha can hear her mom's voice, she can't answer. She feels numb, as if she's in some sort of trance.

"Samantha!" Her mom is holding her face now and is practically yelling at her.

"Mom, relax, I can hear you! It's okay. It just was a lot to take in right then."

Her mom nods in agreement and sighs in relief.

And then suddenly Samantha turns in her chair to face Dr. Jopling.

"Are you okay? Samantha?" Dr. Jopling queries.

"Uh, no. I am most definitely not okay. What exactly are you telling me? I have diabetes. What precisely does this mean?" Samantha's tone is very bitter.

And then came the tears. Samantha feels the wetness and the warmth of her tears starting to brim in her eyes.

Dr. Jopling looks at Samantha. He tries to explain things to her in a kind voice, speaking softly and slowly. "Samantha, I know this is a lot. Okay, so juvenile diabetes or T1D means your body, well, to be exact, your pancreas isn't producing insulin anymore. You will need to give yourself insulin for, well, for the rest of your life. And this disease is called an autoimmune disease, and for some reason—and doctors are still researching the whys—your own body destroyed your insulin-producing cells, thinking they were enemies...."

His eyes are locked in Samantha's as he explains all this to her.

"Now, listen to me for a minute." Dr. Jopling's gaze is still locked on Samantha's eyes. "This news is very overwhelming right now. I understand this completely. I have had to share this diagnosis with many families over the years, and it never gets any easier. You've got one job today, and that's for you and your parents to go downtown to the Dallas Children's Hospital, right now. You'll be admitted and taken to the third floor—the endocrinology floor—and then you'll spend a few days getting regulated and learning how to care for yourself. I'll call right now and let them know you're coming. The endocrine staff, those are the people that care for T1 diabetics, are marvelous. I am very sorry, Samantha. I know this isn't what you were expecting to hear today. I would like to say to you that eventually, this will all work out and be okay, and I know it will, but I know that you don't know that yet. So, for right now, I'll say this. We need to take this one day at a time."

The shock is evident on Samantha's face. All she can say is a quiet, "Okay." Samantha is now staring at the wall. She's taking all of Dr. Jopling's words into her mind, which isn't doing so well right now with this news.

I have a disease? A chronic and autoimmune disease? I was seriously hoping when I came in that this sickness crap would be an easy fix, and I'd go on with my life. But... guess not! I have T1 diabetes?

Samantha lets her thoughts jumble around in her brain like clothes in a dryer until she can sort them out. Now, she can hear her mom and Dr. Jopling talking to each other softly before he leaves the room. Samantha is trying very hard not to listen, which is impossible, but she does hear Dr. Jopling say he will call to check on her in a day or so. Samantha also hears the doctor ask her mom if anyone has an autoimmune disease on either side of their family. Her mom answers in the negative.

As soon as Dr. Jopling leaves, Samantha's mom turns towards her. Samantha senses her mom is looking at her and looks at her mom. Neither one of them can say anything at that moment because what can her mom say? What can Samantha say? There just aren't any words to put out there. Talking would have to come later.

For now, her mom pulls Samantha into a hug. Samantha tries to reciprocate but feels like she's fallen through the ice and is stuck in a frozen lake. Her mom can sense that Samantha is not up to much, so she simply opens the room door and gestures for her to follow.

Samantha feels numb as if she's not actually here experiencing all of this. It's like she's watching this story, her story, all unfold from a camera lens. She can see herself walking along in a dazed state of being. Barely blinking. Samantha slowly walks forward, following her mom like some crazed zombie who can't even think a clear thought! Her mind can't grasp what she's just been told to her. She can't find any logic to any of it. If she were in a book, there would be a scribble of black above her head—like in the Pigeon books—cause she's got nada, zero, nothing, zip!

Samantha and her mom pass the check-out desk, and her mom stops to get the information they'll need when they get to the Dallas

Children's Hospital. Then, they continue forward. Her mom opens the exit door. Samantha follows like her mom in her dazed state, and the next thing she knows, they're by their car. Her mom opens the passenger side door and helps Samantha get in. Samantha climbs into the car. She is aware that her mom has gone 'round and opened the driver's side and gets herself in. Samantha subconsciously buckles her seat belt, and her mom starts the car.

Then she hears her mom call her dad. It is a short, somber conversation, from what she can grasp. Not a lot of explanation, just her mom answering yes and no to her dad's questions.

Samantha continues to be deep in thought as she blankly stares out the window. Clouds have rolled in, and a soft pitter-patter of rain droplets begin to fall from the now darkened sky. Rain is sparse in summer in Texas, but it definitely happens, and to Samantha, it's as if the sky is crying with her in her somber, stunned state of being.

7

"We'll go by the house, Samantha, and pick up some clothes and toiletries and head downtown, okay? Honey, can you hear me?"

Samantha nods yes with her head. Words won't come out of her mouth. Nope. Not one bit. Her phone vibrates in her lap. It's Jules. Samantha quickly reads her text.

Jules: *"Where are you? Are we hanging out tonight with Bo and Rocco?"*

"Mom!" Samantha's voice sounds crackly and whiney as if she hasn't talked much. "It's Jules. I don't know what to say to her!"

"Okay, hold on, um… oh! Tell her we are taking a quick weekend trip. Yeah, I'll text Rocco and tell him what's going on. Is that okay with you?"

"Sure. Just tell him to say nothing to Bo or Jules. Please, Mom."

"Of course. Of course. Whatever you want, sweetie."

Samantha: *"Hey, sorry, my family and I planned an impromptu weekend getaway, and we will most likely be out of cell range—going to the countryside. Text you when I'm home, cool?"*

Jules: *"Of course, miss you already"*

Samantha: *"Ditto"*

Samantha thinks she heard from Dr. Jopling that she and her mom would be in the hospital for about three days, which calculates to be about when she should be home.

THREE DAYS? UGH! What will I be doing for three days? My head hurts, I'm thirsty, and I feel really crappy, so let's hope someone can help me to feel better and soonish!

Mom decides not to pull into their garage but parks in their driveway instead because they'll be in and out pretty quickly. Samantha slowly gets out of their SUV. She closes her door and wanders in through the now-open garage.

She opens the door and sees Rocco first. He's still in his lifeguard outfit, so Samantha assumes he's just coming home from work, and Janey and Dad are home, too. She sees them next, sitting on the family room couches. They come over to greet Samantha and Mom as they enter the kitchen.

"Hey, sis," Rocco says softly. "I'm sorry." There's a catch in his voice.

Samantha looks up and smiles weakly at Rocco. He's about five inches taller than her and getting really tall. She has to stand on her tippy toes to reach his shoulders. He comes toward her and gives her a long hug. She accepts his hug but can only weakly wrap her arms around him. She feels zapped of all her energy.

Next, Janey approaches Samantha and hugs her around the waist. She looks down at her adorable and precious little sister and tries to give her a genuine smile.

"I'm sorry, Sammie."

"Thanks, sweetie. I'll figure it out."

I hope!

Dad walks toward her now and pulls Samantha into a big bear hug. He is tall and cuddly like a big teddy bear anyways. He pulls back and looks into her eyes. "I'm sorry, kiddo."

Samantha looks at him and immediately bursts into tears. Her dad pulls her back in for another hug. Then, Mom, Janey, and Rocco join in for a nice group hug. They all stay like this for a bit. They start to break apart from their lovely hug.

Samantha appreciates it and feels slightly encouraged.

"Janey, Rocco, and I will come down and see you on Friday night, okay?"

Samantha nods and gives her dad a small smile.

"Come on, sweetie. Let's go and pack up a few things to bring with us, and we'll be on our way." Mom takes Samantha's hand and leads her out of the kitchen. She sniffs, grabs a few tissues to wipe her wet eyes, and shuffles up the stairs.

What do you pack to go to the hospital anyway?

She grabs her hairbrush, some makeup, her toothbrush, phone charger, and two pairs of sweats and T-shirts. She's already wearing a pair of sandals with some shorts and a simple T-shirt. She gets three pairs of her unmentionables.

"My sketchbook!" Samantha yells to herself. She grabs her sketchbook and her bag of pens/colored markers. She throws everything into her small duffle bag.

"Samantha, you ready?"

"Coming, Mom," Samantha says resolutely.

8

IT TAKES ABOUT FORTY-FIVE MINUTES TO GET TO THE DALLAS Children's Hospital. Samantha and her mom will be the only two learning and getting trained at the hospital for the next few days. Their drive down is silent. Samantha can feel the anxiety emanating from her and her mom. No music. No talking.

What do we even say to each other right now?

Samantha must have dozed off because as she blinked, she saw the well-lit Children's Hospital sign coming up on the right of them, almost taunting her as her mom pulls into the parking lot.

Welp! Whether I'm ready or not, here I go!

Her mom finds a fairly close parking spot and parks their SUV. They both turn and look at each other. Grasping their hands, and with a continued lack of words, their locked eyes on each other imply: let's do this! Samantha and her mom grab their duffel bags and close the car doors. They walk slowly to the ER entrance. Apparently, Dr. Jopling told her mom to do it this way so Samantha could get

47

checked in quicker since it was nearly 6:00 P.M. A nice male nurse takes Samantha's information and then calls for the endocrinologist nurse on shift to come down and meet her and her mom to take them to the third floor.

"Hey there, Samantha! My name is Beth. I'm going to be your first training nurse. And you must be Mom?" Nurse Beth takes Samantha's hand in hers and shakes it.

"Hi. Yes. I'm Samantha's mom, Annie Hansen." Her mom takes Nurse Beth's extended hand and shakes it, too.

"Let's get upstairs, and I'll fill you both in on what these next few days will look like."

Samantha and her mom nodded in agreement. The elevator ride is silent but quick.

"Okay, so this area here is for our newly diagnosed kiddos with T1D—type 1 diabetes. You ladies will be here in room 3021."

Samantha and her mom follow Nurse Beth to the room. It's a short jaunt, but Samantha is feeling a bit anxious.

This is who I am now—a newly diagnosed type 1 diabetic. What the...?

"Okay, I'll let you both get settled. Samantha, you can put your belongings on this shelf beside your bed. Mom, you can have that area back there." Beth points to an area at the back of the room. "Oh, and Samantha, I need you to wear this attractive blue gown. Mom, here's a bag for all of Samantha's clothes she's wearing now."

She hands the bag to Samantha's mom and turns back to Samantha. "You won't have to wear this for the whole two and a half days you'll be here. I promise! Just for now, as we get your blood sugar level lowered. I'll give you both about ten minutes or so, and I'll be back!"

"Thank you, Nurse Beth," my mom says as Beth turns and walks out of the room. Samantha nods her head and grabs the very unattractive gown. She sneers at it. "Cute, isn't it? Oh, do you think I keep my bra and undies on? Cause I'm gonna."

"Probably. If there's an issue, Nurse Beth will tell us."

Samantha proceeds to take off the outfit she's had on all day and hands each of her clothing items to her mother to stuff into the large, clear plastic bag Nurse Beth gave her mom. Samantha is now dressed in the super attractive blue cotton hospital gown and has her mom help to tie the ties in the back. Her feet are now clad in the fuzzy blue footsies given to her by Nurse Beth, too, so her feet don't get cold.

Her mom is sitting as close as she can to the bed, having pulled over a chair to be ready to hold Samantha's hand whenever needed. Samantha lies in the bed, quietly staring up at the ceiling in her room, as they wait for Nurse Beth to come in and get them started on their "training," whatever that means. As she's lying there, her mind fills with swirling, whirling thoughts going around and around in Samantha's bright right now, like she's watching the water in a sink as it goes spinning down a drain.

Okay, okay, okay! It's time to talk myself down off the edge! I am so overwhelmed right now. I don't know if I need to cry. Or maybe I need to scream? How is it that as of today at around 4:00 P.M., I now have a chronic disease called juvenile diabetes or Type 1 diabetes (T1D for short), and it's also something called an autoimmune disease, which means my own freaking body attacked itself? That in itself is so confusing. And actually, it's really dumb. Why would my body do that to itself?? And I've got to be here for TWO AND A HALF DAYS? What the heck am I going to say to Bo? Jules? I guess I'll say the same thing to Bo if he texts, as I did to Jules, Argh. I need to talk to Rocco. He will help me work through all of this. And speaking of THIS. THIS SITUATION is super dumb. So embarrassing, actually. What the heck do I say next week to both Jules and Bo? Oh, hey guys, so by the way, do you remember I complained about a stomachache? Well, guess what? I just got diagnosed today with a chronic disease, and it's also an autoimmune disease, so there's that! I mean, who wants to hang with someone who has a disease? I feel broken right now, and maybe I am broken! I feel confused. I feel frustrated, too. I don't even know what to think about any of this other than I am still feeling very crappy. One bright spot is that my mom is here with me, and I do really like Nurse Beth. She's awesome. Wow, this is a lot to take in.

Samantha closes her eyes, brooding over her current situation.

Then, she and her mom hear a soft knock on the door to her hospital room.

"Come in," Samantha says quietly.

"Good! Thanks for changing into that cute gown." Beth gives us both an eye-roll. "Now, the first thing we're going to do, Samantha and Annie, is we need to test Samantha's blood sugar again. She's been feeling sick because her blood sugar is super high. When you have to go to the bathroom a lot, and you always feel hungry, those are signs of diabetes mellitus. Your brain thinks you're starving because your insulin is not breaking down your food like it should. Did you get all that? Let me say it again. We eat food. Our pancreas has insulin that spurs out and breaks down our food into workable energy and if your body doesn't make it, you need to put insulin into your body. We're gonna check again now and see where you're at, and then we'll give you insulin slowly to bring you down into a normal range, which is between 80 and 120. That means if I check someone's blood sugar anytime they come into a doctor's office, it should fall between 80–120 if their pancreas is functioning properly."

"We did just do this a bit ago with Dr. Jopling. It was 690 I think," Samantha tells Beth.

"Right, I think I saw that on your info sheet. Just going to do it again so I have it recorded on my machine here."

Beth did everything so quickly as Marie did. And before either Samantha or her mom could even say a word, the machine beeped.

BEEP

725

"Yikes! So, that's just a little bit out of range!" Beth giggles, which makes Samantha and her mom giggle, releasing the cortisol flowing through their bodies and brains for the last few hours.

"Just a bit," her mom says, laughing. Samantha gives a little smile, too.

"Okay, I'm going to set you up with an IV of insulin. I told you just a few minutes ago that we want to do this slowly because you are so high. We don't want to bring you down into the normal range rapidly. So, if you will both sit back and Mom, you can put your chair close over by Samantha's bed and then I will get this set up for you, and it will take quite a few hours to get you down into a normal range. Here's the TV remote. I also have coloring books or books to read because we have a great system for kids/teens when they come to the hospital. People donate toys, coloring books, books, movies, etc., so that you can keep yourself entertained while you're here. I'll be back in about fifteen minutes with all the IV stuff, etc., okay? Oh, do you need any books or movies?"

"I'm good. I brought my sketchbook, but thanks, Nurse Beth."

"Okay, ladies, I'll be back!"

Samantha and her mom watch as Nurse Beth leaves the room. Samantha immediately starts talking to her mom.

"Holy crap, Mom, that is so high! I guess that makes a lot of sense now, as to why I've been feeling so awful."

"I absolutely agree! You poor thing. I am so sorry that this is all happening to you right now. I'm glad they know what they're doing to get your blood sugar down slowly, and I hope that as it does, you will start to feel better, and then you can kind of process all of this a little bit more as we go through your weekend of training. What do you think?"

"I sure hope so, Mom. I really hope so! I was lying there after I put on my gown, and so many thoughts were spinning in my mind. I'm very, very overwhelmed, but maybe you're right. As my blood sugar decreases, I hope to feel better." Samantha's smiles at her mom. "Oh, Mom, will you hand me my canvas bag? I brought my sketchbook, markers, and pens."

"Oh, that's a great idea. And do you want to call Rocco? He's been dying to talk with you."

"Yes, for sure. I've been dying to talk with Rocco, too! I don't think I can even concentrate enough to watch anything."

"Yeah, me neither. I did bring a book to read. I don't want to text anyone except Dad and Rocco right now."

"Yes, please. I'm still trying to deal with this. I don't need anyone's pity or weird comments."

"Agreed."

Samantha pulls out her sketchbook, grabs her pencil bag full of pens and markers, and begins sketching for a few minutes to calm herself. She then picks up her phone to call Rocco. She dials his number, and he picks up after one ring.

9

"Samantha? Oh my gosh, are you okay?"

"Well, I mean, I figured out what's been going on, I'm sure mom told you."

"Yeah, like what the heck?"

"I know. A chronic disease? T1D, and I have to give myself insulin? Right now, my brain is on overload, so Nurse Beth said for me to just chill while my blood sugar comes down. Rocco, it was 725! That's ridiculously high!! I guess the normal range is 80 to 120!"

"Duuuude, you knocked it out of the park, Sis, sheesh!"

"Yeah, you know me! Always trying for a high score on anything I do." They both laugh.

"K, so tell me what's happening right now," he says. "It's way weird to have you gone for so long. I mean you hang with Jules all day every day, but you're always home to sleep! It's almost 9:00 P.M., and I keep looking for you! Even if I'm gone, we both end up in the tv room together, ya know?"

"Uh, yeah, I know! So, I had to put on that dumb, unattractive blue hospital nightgown. So attractive, ha, ha. And Nurse Beth is going to start my IV here pretty quickly. I needed to change first. Mom is reading a book and I'm sure texting Daddio. Then, this IV full of insulin will be a slow drip to bring down my blood sugar. You can't do it quickly, they say. It takes time, so we're hopeful for it to be in range by the morning. How's Janey? What did you guys tell her?"

"Dad dished up her favorite ice cream, sat us both down, and told us what was happening with you. Janey, the-ever-drama-queen, asked if you were going to die, so, wow, Dad had to settle her down with that thought process."

"Poor kiddo. I was worried about that. Oh, Jules and Bo texted me, and I told them we had taken an impromptu family trip for the weekend. So, don't say anything okay? I will do it...." Samantha sounds less than confident.

"Of course, Sis, of course. Do you think you'll be able to sleep at all?"

"No idea. At this point, I have to pee every five minutes and then someone will come in every few hours to check my blood sugar and vitals, so probably not too much!"

"Crud, sorry. Okay, so, listen to me. If you feel the slightest upset, or stressed or anything, I don't care what time it is you text me, okay? And we three will be coming up tomorrow after dinner, okay?"

"Thank you and yay!! And, Rocco, you're my bestest brother ever! Thank you."

"Well, I hope so since I am your only brother. Love you, sis."

Samantha pushes the end button and lies back on her pillow.

BEST BROTHER EVER AND SISTER! I'm so glad I have a good family. What if I didn't? This situation would be so much worse! I can't even imagine!

The night wears on. The IV of insulin drips into her tubing and ever so slowly, her blood sugar is coming down. 725 was super high, thus the slow insulin drip to get Samantha down into the range of 80-180. She tries hard to rest. Beth suggests that if she could do this then, by the next day, she'll be feeling better and more normal to start their full day of instruction. Nurse Beth said she'd be in to teach them a few things to finish the night, and then she'd promise to let them be. It was nearly 10:00 P.M. when Beth knocked and then popped in again.

"Hello lovelies! I'm going to sit here in this chair." Nurse Beth points at another chair in the room and pulls it closer to her mom and Samantha's bed. "And I find the best way to deal with this lifestyle change is just to jump right in. First, I need to explain to you some things before we get started tonight. If your doctor hasn't already told you this, I need to tell you one important thing. Samantha, you will accomplish anything and can do anything that you want to do in your life. I don't want you to fear that you will be impeded by this disease one bit."

After sharing these first thoughts, Beth falls silent and looks at Samantha and her mother. Both looked back at Nurse Beth with tearful eyes. Neither Samantha nor her mother could say anything. They just smiled, wiped their tears, and nodded in the affirmative.

"Okay. First off, let's learn what the heck diabetes mellitus, type 1 diabetes, or juvenile diabetes, is. I know Dr. Jopling gave you the basic information. He's one of the few docs with such good knowledge of this disease, for which I am grateful. Anyway, yes doggone it, it is a chronic disease, which means it's with you until you croak. And it's an autoimmune disease, too, which means your immune system attacks healthy cells.

Beth takes a breath and continues. "With T1D—and this is what I'll be calling it from here on out—your body attacks your healthy pancreas and destroys your insulin-producing cells. Yeah. Yikes! I know all of this has been a lot to take in and believe it or not, medical scientists and researchers still don't know why the body does this."

Samantha feels like she can finally say something now. "Wow. That's so weird. So, what I am to understand is this: T1D is both a chronic and an autoimmune disease? Dang. So how did I even get this?" Samantha's query is visible on her face as she looks very confused.

"Good question! Research has shown that those who get a T1D diagnosis are predisposed to the gene for it. And it varies as to what can trigger it. Stress. Trauma. Sickness. And so forth."

"I mean, I guess I could've been stressed. But no, not really. And I haven't been sick. I've been sick because of how I've been feeling. So weird. So, so weird. Like I was just fine a few months ago and now I've got a chronic disease? Like what?"

"I agree. It is a weird thing. And being older, you're going to understand a lot more about all of this. So that's why I want to be very thorough as I explain what is going on with your body, what's going to happen, and what you will learn to do to take care of yourself. Now, y'all try and get some rest! I'm off until tomorrow P.M."

"Thank you!" both Samantha and her mom say in unison. As soon as Beth leaves,

Samantha lets out a really long and full-of-feels sigh.

Sighhhhhhhhh

"Okay, wow, that was a lot of info!" Samantha looks at her mom when she says this.

"Yeah, it was, but I do feel more informed," she agrees.

"Yeah, I agree, but it's still a lot to digest, ya know?"

"For sure. My brain is swirling a bit." Her mom laughs lightly.

"Yep, that's how I'm feeling. Sheesh!"

"I'm going to go out and call Dad and then come in and try to sleep a bit. Does that sound okay to you?" her mom asks her.

"Yes, of course, Mom! And Mom? Thank you for being here with me!" Samantha feels tears threatening to gather in her eyes, but she manages to keep them at bay.

"Darlin', I wouldn't have it any other way. Try to sleep if you can. I love you," her mom says as she leans down and plants a fabulous kiss on her forehead.

Samantha watches as her mom grabs her phone and leaves the room. She puts aside her sketchbook, marker bag, and cell phone and tries to make a big effort to relax and sleep if she can.

Samantha has her eyes closed, yet sleep isn't coming. It is around 11:30 P.M. now. Her mom has finally fallen asleep, and Samantha continues to give her best effort, but her mind continues to be a swirling whirlpool of thoughts.

How did this ever happen to me? How hard will it be to care for myself? Will I even understand HOW to care for my blood sugars or whatever I am

supposed to be doing? What will others think of me? Jules? Bo? My family? This is not happening to me! This just can't be right!

Since entering the hospital yesterday, it had all been a whirlwind of blood tests to see what her blood sugar level number was 725. That was way too high. Normal functioning pancreases put everyone at about 80-120. Then there was training, talking, more training, and so on. Her diagnosis of T1D yesterday seems unreal. She's found out that this T1D is a chronic disease, meaning it would never go away. It was also an autoimmune disease, meaning Samantha's own body had thought there was an invasion in her pancreas and had attacked the insulin-making cells. Now, her life as she once knew it would never be the same—ever. In two days, she will go home to a different and challenging lifestyle.

The tears came more freely now. She was so afraid! Could she die? Would she be able to do everyday things? What would her friends say?

So many questions and concerns continue to fill her mind, so she decides to put on her headphones, wishing that this will all go away amidst her tunes. Samantha's mind continued to whirl, but the music calmed her and soothed her fears, and she finally drifted off to sleep at some point. That was until around 3:00 A.M. when another nurse came in. Nurse Beth got off shift around 11:00 P.M. so she could return in the daytime for the next two or three days.

10

SAMANTHA IS COMPLETELY ASLEEP when she feels someone shaking her shoulder.

"Hey Samantha, it's Jeff. I'm sorry to wake you up, but I must check your vitals and blood sugar. Is that okay?"

"Sure, of course," Samantha says groggily.

"Okay. I'll prick your finger now, but starting in the morning, I will have you be in charge of your pricks."

Samantha's eyes widen.

"You will be just fine. I promise. You'll get the hang of all of them quickly. I promise you."

Samantha just nods and lies her head back on her pillow.

"354. Good. You're coming down nicely. I filled your hospital cup with ice water. I need you to continue to drink water as your blood sugar levels come down, and we nurses will continue to refill it for you. Drinking water is one of the best ways to help you feel better when your blood sugar is high, as we call it."

Samantha took her cup from him and swilled as much water as she could. She'd had to go to the bathroom a million times already, so what's a little more water going to do?

"Thanks, Jeff," Samantha says, more awake now.

"You're welcome. Your vitals are good, too. So that's terrific. See if you can get more rest before I return around 6:00 A.M."

Samantha gives him a thumbs-up, closes her eyes, and drifts off quickly. A short few hours later, she's dead to the world asleep, but she thinks she hears her name called. Slowly, she opens her eyes.

"Hey Samantha. It's Jeff again. I'm just going to do a quick blood check."

Samantha gives a barely audible groan in agreement but keeps her eyes closed.

"265. Good, good. By 8:00 am, you should be near the normal range of 70-150. Excellent. K, I'll be back around 8:00 am."

"K," barely comes out as Samantha keeps her eyes shut and is asleep in like two minutes.

Samantha sleeps for another two hours until Nurse Beth comes in to wake her up.

"Samantha, it's Beth. I'm sorry to wake you, but I need you to do a blood check and teach you how to count and estimate your carbs for breakfast."

Samantha manages to open her eyes slowly. She looks over at her mom, who's also waking up. Samantha reaches over and grabs her blood checker monitor. She cocks the lancet and pushes the button against her pointer finger.

Oh, that hurts. I hope I'll get used to the pricks and that they will eventually stop hurting as much.

185

Samantha shows Nurse Beth the screen.

"185 is a much better number. I hope you're feeling better." Nurse Beth grins at Samantha.

"I actually do, yeah. Thank goodness! I am starving though."

"I bet you are starving. Poor girl! Okay, I will remove the insulin drip IV, and you'll be going on shots. Now, if you both want to freshen up and get dressed, I'll be right back to help you order your breakfast, Samantha. Annie, I can order your meals alongside Samantha while you're here if that works for you. I'll just make a note on the computer so you can pay the tab at the end. Does that work for you?"

"Absolutely!" Her mom smiles as she says this. Samantha is grateful her mom isn't a high-maintenance person.

"Here are two sheets showing you both what the schedule will be for the next two days." Beth hands the papers to Samantha and her mom. They both take a minute to look it over.

This is what the daily schedule will be:

8:30 A.M.: Blood check

8:30 A.M.: Breakfast, calculate carbs and insulin shot.

class

10:00 A.M.: Snack and insulin (if over fifteen carbs)

class

Noon, lunch and insulin shot

class

2:00 P.M.: Snack and insulin

Class

6:00 P.M.: Dinner and insulin

7:00 P.M.: Nighttime snack

Blood checks before each meal and before each snack

3:00 A.M. and 6:00 A.M. checks

Start all over again at 8:30 A.M.

Wowwww. It's going to be a busy day! But what else should a teen girl be doing on a now non-rainy, beautiful, sunny Texas summer day other than be in the hospital?

When Samantha performs her first blood check before breakfast this morning, she doesn't do very well. The prick doesn't yield enough blood, so she has to crank up the lancet a little bit more. Then she pricks her finger again, and a good drop of blood comes out. Samantha puts it close to the test strip and watches as it sucks up her blood. It does a complete countdown for about a minute, and then she hears a beep, which will be her constant friend for the next while.

Samantha and her mom get themselves cleaned up and ready for a long day of training and education. Nurse Beth comes back in and walks Samantha and her mom through the process of carb counting and what Samantha's scale of insulin doses would be according to the number of carbs Samantha potentially will eat for her meals… until she can qualify for the continuous glucose monitor, or CGM, which will check your blood sugar automatically.

But for now, Samantha needs to give herself shots and she needs to check her blood sugar so she can get used to what that means, and she needs to learn how to understand blood sugar numbers. Training on day two consists of understanding how she eats. When the blood sugar spikes, insulin breaks it down and turns it into energy for our body to use. And then she learned that when her insulin isn't working, how that affects her body. That is why her blood sugar was so high. She had no insulin to break down her food/carbohydrates.

I mean, it's not like I even gave a thought about my pancreas nor whether it was spurting insulin out or not… ever before! And now, my whole life has changed, and that will now be my daily goal: match my insulin dose to my carbohydrate intake. Wow, that is really all I can think of, just WOW!

Samantha and her mom have different subjects and nurses who came in and out throughout the first day. Their brains become so full of information that they are absolutely exhausted after day one of training! They'd eaten dinner, and Samantha had done all her blood checks, shots, etc., so they were ready to rest for the night. Samantha decided to lie down and just relax. She and her mom were so tired that her mom texted Samantha's dad to tell them all to come Saturday night instead of tonight.

What a day! I learned what it means to check your blood sugars and how to treat a low and a high blood glucose number. I was able to prick my fingers all by myself throughout the day and I gave myself insulin shots. Tomorrow, the nurses will show my mom and me a PowerPoint presentation that explains how food spikes blood sugar and how insulin breaks it down.

Doing my own shots and blood checks for the rest of the day went way better than I'd thought after I got the hang of it all! The calculating of the carbs is a drag, but I got this app called MyNetDiary so thankfully, it can do it on the app.

Beth taught Mom and me how to calculate food without the app first, though, which was good. There are some in-app purchases, but what I need for now is free.

Blood checks are still painful. I'm looking forward to building up those calluses. Also, I learned how to draw up the insulin from the vial and give myself shots. Mom gave me a shot, too, and we will teach Dad and Rocco. Beth says making this disease a family affair goes a long way and will help me emotionally deal with it all better. I'm slowly improving my technique of giving myself shots, which is a plus.

It's dinner time, so more blood checks, calculating, and a shot! Beth taught us about a CGM—continuous glucose monitor system—which tests my blood sugar continuously through a patch with a tiny needle inserted into my skin. Those numbers are then sent automatically to my phone, and on an app, I can see my blood sugar, and it will tell me to pump up if I am low or correct with insulin if I'm high. I can be eligible to get this in three to four months if I keep my blood sugars within range as much as I can. Then! And this is big news, too—after I get the CGM, then in a few more months after that, I can get an insulin pump, which means NO MORE SHOTS! Beth told Mom and me that they teach everyone how to do everything without the CGM or pump because technology can fail, and I will need to know how to care for myself without all the bells and whistles.

BZZZZ

Samantha's phone vibrates and breaks her train of many thoughts.

It's Bo!

Bo: *"Hey, Samantha! Just checking in. We all have been hanging out so much that I am getting withdrawals from you three, ha ha"*

HE'S SO SWEET! I MISS HIM TOO! AND JULES! UGH. I DON'T LIKE BEING deceitful to my friends.

SAMANTHA: *"HEY, BO! I'M SO SORRY I COULDN'T RESPOND EARLIER. WE were out and about as a family. But thanks for texting! We're having a great weekend. I should be home by late Sunday night. What's up with you this weekend?"*

Samantha knows full well that Bo is probably so bored because she and Rocco are "gone," and it's not like Bo and Jules would hang out. Bo had checked in with her earlier, but Samantha had been so inundated with training that she couldn't respond.

Bo: *"Just hanging with my little sister and parents. We went to a movie today and out to eat together. Church tomorrow, and probs will take a walk to the park—nothing too crazy. Well, gotta go"*

Samantha: *"Cool! Bye, thanks for checking in"*

SAMANTHA COULDN'T SAY, "SEE YOU MONDAY," OR, "LET'S HANG OUT," because she didn't know what Monday would be like.

CRAP. THIS SO SUCKS!! I just want to be a NORMAL TEEN!! Now what am I??

Her phone vibrates again. This time it's Jules!

Jules: *"Samantha! Rocco hasn't even texted me for about two days. Should I be concerned?"*

Samantha gives an eye roll to the ceiling.

Samantha: *"Gurl, no, we've been super busy, just chill"*

Jules: *"Okay, okay, just asking. Has Bo texted you?"*

Samantha: *"Yes 2x's"*

Jules: *"Ooooh, fabulous"*

Samantha: *"Again, chill, we're just friends, as are you and Rocco. Let's keep it that way"*

Jules: *"Yes, mother hen ha, ha"*

Samantha: *"Gotta go"*

Jules: *"Byeeeee"*

Samantha puts up her phone and readies herself for bed. She and her mom gratefully called it a day after the before-bedtime blood glucose check, snack, and long-acting insulin through-the-night shot. Samantha puts on her headphones and goes into her happy place. She sets a timer for her music to shut off in about an hour.

As she drifts off to sleep, she looks at her cute mom, who is already fast asleep. Poor thing. Her mom has got to be just as tired as Samantha is!

11

THE NIGHT NURSE did a 3:00 A.M. blood sugar test on Samantha. They'll do it on Sunday at 3:00 A.M., too, and Samantha may have to continue this until the glucose numbers continue in the 70-150 range.

"Rise and shine, Samantha!" Nurse Beth chirps sweetly like a little singing bird.

"Already?" Samantha groans. She sees her mom stretching and standing up while folding her bedding. Samantha gets out of her bed and walks to the bathroom. She was able to wear normal clothes yesterday and can wear them today, too.

Hallelujah.

"Good morning, sleepy head! Ugh, I look awful!" Samantha laughs at herself and analyzes her crazy hair and very tired-looking face. She attempts to wake herself up by washing her face, brushing her hair and teeth and applying some makeup, dresses, then uses the toilet, which, thankfully, her excessive potty adventures have subsided.

Now, according to her training, when she has a high, she'll have to use the restroom more, but otherwise, she should be normal-ish again. Samantha, who usually never wears sweats, etc., chose to bring sweatshirts, tees, leggings, slides, and socks. For the last day and a half, she has pulled her hair up in a messy bun, not caring about how she looked one bit, which verifies the amount of emotional stress she is under because she always cares about how she looked. Deciding to put on makeup seemed to pep her whole persona up, and that felt good and more normal to Samantha.

Day two training taught Samantha and her mom about a period of time right after a diagnosis that Samantha is still in, called "the honeymoon." This period means her body will still produce insulin but sporadically. It will be in spurts until her pancreas' insulin-producing cells are completely dead. Sounds very morbid, but that's the gist of it.

After the honeymoon, she can be on a more regular shot regimen and be able to regulate her blood sugar, and then she should be able to work toward getting her CGM. Most of all, Samantha can then move toward getting an insulin pump.

Samantha and her mom learn a bit about CGM and the insulin pump. More info will be divulged to them when Samantha gets approved and trained for the CGM. One of the best little tidbits of information Samantha and her mom learn is that any snack that is fifteen grams of carbs or lower does not require insulin! Like day one, day two was chalked full of a whole slew of so much more information!

Another day of blood checking, calculating, and shots brought Samantha to after dinner on day two!

Phew! I am beat! My brain feels like mush. I surely hope I can remember all of this, but at least the various nurses told us that we could call the diabetes hotline at any time for assistance. I am glad for this option.

Samantha's ears perk up as she hears familiar voices at her door — Janey, Rocco, and Dad— trickle into her room for their visit.

"Oh my gosh! I am so glad to see you three!!"

There was a collective, "us too," as they all hugged and visited. Her mom kissed her head and said she wouldn't be long. She was heading home for a couple of hours.

"Mom, please take your time! You've barely slept up here, and I appreciate you being here with me," Samantha says to her mother as she waves goodbye to them all.

"I wouldn't have it any other way, sweetheart. Do you need anything at the house?"

"Nah, I'm good, but thanks!"

Everyone says goodbye to her mom, and they continued to visit.

"Samantha, are you sick?" Janey asks innocently.

"Well, yes and no. I was very sick until nurses Beth and Jeff got my blood sugar under control, it's called. Now I'm feeling so much better! So, basically, if my blood sugars get too low or too high, I will feel sick. I've got to try to keep them in a range. Does that make sense?"

"Sort of." Janey has a look of concern on her sweet face.

"Come sit by me, Janey."

Janey pulls a chair close by Samantha.

"I have been very scared, too. I didn't understand everything that had happened to me in the past two days, but the nurses and doctors here have been marvelous. They've explained everything about diabetes and the science of insulin, including how it deals with my food, etc. I feel less overwhelmed and want you to know I need your help!"

"You will? What can I do?"

"Well, there will be many times when my blood sugars will be too low or too high like I said a little bit ago. Those are times when I'll need juice when I'm low or big cups of water if I'm high. Do you think you could do that for me?"

"Oh yes, Sammie! I'd love to help you!"

Samantha gives her little sister a big hug.

"Thank you, Janey."

Samantha smiled, and Rocco took Janey's hand to go get something from the vending machine so she and her dad could talk. "We will take a jaunt around and look for some treats. We will be back in a bit!" Rocco smiled widely at Samantha. She was the luckiest sister.

"Thank you, Rocco. You and I can talk more when y'all come back."

Dad took the same chair that Janey had recently sat in. He looked at Samantha with his soft, kind eyes.

"So, how are you feeling about everything today? You've got one more day and a half of training, right?"

"Sure do. And it's been a lot. Wow. I feel better tonight than I did this morning. Man, oh, man. I was feeling a feeling of self-pity and doubt and all of those kinds of things. Yuck. I detest feeling those things."

"And can anyone blame you? This is a lot to take in in just a few days. Wow. Mom has shared all of the training you two have been doing. Dr. Swaneyard wants us all to know as much as we can to be a support to you. I was very impressed with this thinking."

"Dr. Swaneyard is the best! He's been so stellar. So kind. And so encouraging. I am glad that he said that this is a family affair. I need you guys." And before she knew it, tears were streaming down her face. Again.

"I'm so sorry, sweet girl. So sorry. You've been super brave, though, and that's not an easy thing to do with so many unknowns."

Samantha stands up, and her dad does, too, and he holds tightly in a really good bear hug—the kind that makes her feel safe and at home.

"Hey, can we come in?" Rocco knocks lightly on the door of her room.

Samantha and her dad sit back down, and Samantha calls to them. "Yep! Come on in." She wipes her face for like the millionth time!

"Look what I got, Sammie! An Oreo pack and a teeny milk!"

For some reason, this makes everyone laugh and breaks Samantha's tearful state.

"I love you, Janey girl." Samantha hugs her cutie little sister.

Their dad speaks up. "Janey, let's check out the art display we saw on the first floor and let Samantha and Rocco visit, okay?"

"Okay," Janey says reluctantly, giving her dad an eye roll. "Big people talk."

They all laugh again. Samantha returns to sitting crisscross applesauce in her hospital bed. Rocco, now the third occupant of the chair next to her bed, sits and begins to ask Samantha so many questions!

"Okay, so let me get this straight. You have a chronic autoimmune disease, and you have to dose yourself with insulin and count your carbs. Oh, and blood check?"

"Well. When you put it like that it's a bit much, ha, ha."

"Ha, ha. Yeah, just a bit. Well, if anyone can do it, you can, sis. I know you can, and we will all help you acclimate to it all."

She takes Rocco's hand and squeezes it. "Thank you. That means a lot, because I feel like I'm drowning in a storm-ridden ocean because of my many emotions right now!"

"Understandably so! This really is a little life-altering."

"Yeah, sure is."

Their dad and Janey walk back into Samantha's room. "Samantha, you should see all of the cool art stuff!" Janey says excitedly. "It was so, so cool!"

"Awesome. I will check it out tomorrow. Nurse Jeff and Nurse Beth say we will have more training tomorrow, and then I can go home!"

"Oh good!" Samantha's dad says. "We miss you at home." He looks at his phone. "Okay, guys, I just got a text from Mom. She's parking and is coming back up to the third floor. Samantha, we look forward to seeing you at home tomorrow!" He kisses her on her forehead. Then, both Janey and Rocco hug her.

"I love you all! Thanks for coming up. I was feeling super overwhelmed and some serious self-pity today." Samantha shares this with her family.

Her mom walks into the room smelling delightful before hugging Dad, Rocco, and Janey goodbye. Samantha almost tears up, watching the three of them leave her room. But she is certainly glad her mom is back! She's been Samantha's rock this weekend.

"Yay, Mom, you're back! I bet a shower was super nice at home, yeah?"

Actually, it was the best—not gonna lie—but I made it as quick as possible with an hour and a half of travel time. I didn't want to be gone too long, but I knew you were fine with everyone here with you. How was your visit?"

"Great. I really needed it. I talked with Dad first and then with

Rocco. It was very healing, I guess, is what I'd say. I'm glad they stayed for a good long while. I needed to see them all."

"Good! I was hoping it would cheer you up some, too. I'm sorry, Samantha. I know these past few days have all been just so much to learn and take in."

"That's exactly what I was saying to Rocco. I still feel like things are overwhelming."

* * *

"IT'S SUNDAY! YAY! TODAY, I CAN GO HOME... WELL, I HOPE I CAN GO home!" Samantha is saying this with glee as she's fixing her bed.

She'd been up early packing up her duffel and is already dressed and ready for the day. Since coming in Thursday night and getting her blood sugar lowered into a more normal range, she's continued to feel better physically. Her blood sugar numbers overall had been pretty stable since then. Now, emotionally, she is still feeling super overwhelmed and slightly vulnerable and still very abnormal. Samantha is sitting on her bed, waiting for Nurse Beth to come in and discharge her.

"Well, look at you! I think someone wants to get home today!" Nurse Beth smiles at Samantha and continues. "Samantha, I am super proud of you!! You've mastered every skill you need to go home later this morning. Now, I know you're going to say, but Beth, how do I take care of myself? I'm here to say you can and will be able to care for your diabetes, manage it, and live life. I have already seen your determination and hard work. You've been very diligent in all of the training sessions. And, as Dr. Swaneyard told you yesterday, 'The more you check, the more you know!' Until you get that CGM, there will be sporadic checks. Please remember that you can't guess your blood glucose number!"

Samantha gives Nurse Beth a goofy smile and says, "Duh."

She definitely knows she has her work cut out for her, though, and achieving the CGM and then an insulin pump seem like attainable goals.

"Okay, ladies, I'm going to prepare your paperwork for discharge and get all the supplies to take home with you. You can throw your blue nightgown into that bin over there, and Annie, if you don't mind packing up the rest of her supplies, we can speed up this process."

"Great, thanks, Nurse Beth," Samantha says sweetly. "I appreciate you very much, Beth."

Beth gives Samantha a warm smile and pats her shoulder as she leaves the room.

"Let's get you packed up, sweetie," her mom says. "I just need to use the restroom quickly." She has to use the restroom down the hallway because family members can't use the bathrooms in the patients' rooms.

12

SAMANTHA IS ALL READY, so she sits in a chair to wait and pulls out her sketchbook. She hears a soft knock on her door.

Why would my mom be knocking?

"Come in," Samantha says very softly. She turns around to see her very best friend in the whole wide world, Jules, standing with a gift bag and balloons.

Samantha's face lights up with sheer happiness. "Jules? What? How did you...?" Samantha can't finish her sentence.

Jules smiles back, walks over to Samantha, and hugs her. "Hey Samantha. I know you told your mom not to tell anyone, and she didn't, just so you know, but I happened to drop by your house to return some of your clothes, and since I know your garage code, I let myself in and scared Rocco and Janey half out of their wits! That's when I had a little tete-a-tete with Rocco, and he gave me the low-down." She looks right at Samantha. "You could have told me, you know."

Samantha keeps quiet. She's a little embarrassed that she didn't trust Jules with her diagnosis, but not completely so because it has been so much for her to deal with, let alone involve anyone besides her family.

Jules continues to talk. "I didn't know what to bring you, so I decided on a stuffed bear and a balloon."

"Thank you, Jules," Samantha says quietly.

"Why didn't you tell me… while we were texting yesterday?" Jules asks, perplexed.

"I just couldn't, Jules. I'm very overwhelmed right now. It's all I can do to make it through all I have been learning and taking in. I am sorry. I just want to go home and be normal, which will never happen again," Samantha says, sniffing and wiping small tears from her eyes. "I was in shock. I still am. I'm barely dealing with the info myself, so there was no way I had enough strength to tell you. And all I can think of is how will I tell Bo? He'll think I'm some sick freak!"

"Samantha! I am sure he won't! I promise." Jules tries to sound convincing.

"How can you even know that?" Samantha eyes Jules.

"Well, I can say that with honesty because Bo is a good person, and your brother wouldn't hang with a type of person who wouldn't be kind or understanding of his sister," Jules explains.

"Okay, yeah, that makes sense."

They both sit quietly for a bit. Both girls now have tears in their eyes. While sitting silently, Jules tries to break the sad mood by telling Samantha some of her siblings' crazy and funny stories. This works, and Samantha laughs and laughs and laughs. It's a welcome pleasure.

"Um, Jules?"

"Yes, Samantha?"

"Umm, I don't know how much I can hang out before school starts. Umm, I've got to get my rhythm down of caring for my diabetes. It's a lot right now, but there's a light at the end of the tunnel because I can get trained in about three to four months and get a CGM—a continuous glucose monitor—which will take away the finger pricks! Then, in a few months after that, and when I'm out of my honeymoon period, which means when my insulin-producing cells are basically all dead, then I can qualify for an insulin pump, which means no more shots!"

"Woah! I don't even know what that all means, but it sounds like fantastic news. I am so glad you have that to look forward to. I can't even imagine how you're feeling right now. Of course, you're overwhelmed!"

"That's exactly why... my brain is chalked full of information. That's what I've been doing up here since Thursday night. And yes. It is good news about both the CGM and the insulin pump."

Samantha's mom returns from the restroom. She sees Jules, who comes to hug her. "Thank you for coming, Jules. It means a lot to us both."

"You're welcome, Ms. Annie."

Samantha's mom sits in the same chair she's occupied for their stay at the Children's Hospital and opens her book to read until it's time to leave. The girls continue visiting until Jules's mom texts her, saying she is ready to return home.

"Okay, Samantha, I will check in with you tomorrow, okay?"

"Okay, and Jules, thanks for coming. It means so much to me. I so appreciate it."

"It's my pleasure to visit with my bestie. See you soon!" Jules waves to Samantha and Samantha's mom and leaves the room.

"Well, I needed that visit from Jules," Samantha tells her mom.

"I know you did. Glad it worked out for Jules to come and see you while you're still here."

Jules's visit definitely boosted Samantha's spirits a lot. Although Samantha knew Jules did have a clue what she was dealing with, it was okay. Better to have a supportive friend than not.

"Okay, let's get ready to go home!" Nurse Beth says enthusiastically as she pops back into the room.

"Yes," Samantha says. "It's not that I don't love you, Jeff, and Dr. Swaneyard, but no offense... I want to go home!"

"Of course you do, sweet girl. Okay, in this paperwork, I need you, Annie, to call and set a three-month appt with Dr. Swaneyard," she addresses Samantha's mom. "Samantha, you will see him until you're eighteen every three months and then move up to an adult doctor. We have some great options for you when it comes to that time. For now, get home and get some rest. And take each day one day at a time. I'm serious! You will have some up and down days, but I just need you to keep going forward!"

Samantha gives Beth a huge hug.

"Beth, thank you for everything," Samantha's mom says, hugging Nurse Beth. "We will be forever grateful to you." She smiles and grabs Samantha's duffel bag and her own bag.

"You're welcome. Working with you, teaching you, and getting to know you both this weekend has been a pleasure. Samantha—" Nurse Beth focuses on Samantha now. "Here are your needles, a receptor to put the used needles, vials of test strips, lancets, your insulin, and all the prescriptions you need for these items."

Nurse Beth hands everything to Samantha in a big bag. Samantha takes it and holds it close to her.

My diabetes maintenance life is all in a bag! That is such a weird concept!

"Okay, let me get Jeff to get a wheelchair to take you down. I know. Weird. But it's protocol."

They patiently wait for Nurse Beth as she texts Jeff. He appears promptly with the wheelchair, and Samantha hands her mom the bag of all of her supplies. Beth waves goodbye to them both and watches Samantha enter the wheelchair.

It feels weird to get into the wheelchair again and be wheeled like a helpless and sick person. Samantha's mom walks beside her. The three get onto the elevator and travel to the first-floor lobby. The doors open, and Samantha can see the doors leading to the outdoors! Fresh air… she can't wait to feel the hot sun.

"Let me grab the car. I parked close by. I'll put it right up by the front doors," her mom says as she walks ahead and goes out the automatic doors.

Jeff wheels Samantha right up to the automatic doors, and as they open, the heat washes over Samantha. She's never been so happy to feel the sun on her head and body in her entire young life.

Samantha's mom pulls up right as she and Jeff are at the curb. He helps Samantha get up and out of the wheelchair, then shakes her hand. "Good luck, Samantha. You're gonna do great!"

"Thanks, Jeff!"

Her mom unlocks the door, and Samantha climbs into the car.

"Hallelujah!! I've never been happier to go home in my entire life!" Samantha practically shouts as she buckles her seatbelt.

Mom reaches for Samantha's hand and grabs her hand. "I know, sweetheart. Me too!!"

* * *

OVER THE NEXT FOUR WEEKS, SAMANTHA SEES VERY LITTLE OF BOTH Jules and Bo. It's difficult staving them off, but she keeps making excuses. Samantha can't bring herself to have Jules or Bo watch her blood check or give herself shots. It's just embarrassing, and it's still painful, so watching her grimace is not going ever to be an option. She surely doesn't feel comfortable with anyone knowing about her new lifestyle changes, plus, let's be frank, she's still getting used to this whole new lifestyle herself!

Over the last four weeks of her summer, Samantha tries to get used to the constant blood checks, the shots, and calculating her food. She texts a lot with Bo and Jules but doesn't hang out with them! Rocco helps make excuses for Samantha and ends up not even having Bo come over. Unfortunately for Samantha, that doesn't stop Rocco, Jules, and Bo from hanging together. I mean, Samantha made this choice, and she knew what she was doing. But it still sucks.

While she's adjusting to her diet, blood checks, and insulin, they're all out school shopping, swimming, or going to the movies. Samantha doesn't even want to hear what Rocco or Jules are doing. It hurts Samantha's heart and gives her such bad FOMO.

Since her visit to the hospital, Jules has checked in with Samantha every couple of days, which Samantha appreciates. Bo also checks in, but he doesn't know what's happening with her.

Samantha can't tell if he's convinced of her excuses, but she persists. She isn't ready to share this part of her life with Bo, and she hopes he will have patience with the unknown for now. Samantha pleads with Jules and Rocco to promise they will not tell Bo anything!

When the time is right, she will tell him.

13

One Week Before School Starts

Rocco has gone to pick up Bo and Jules, and they are going to the movies AGAIN! Samantha is over all of this. Since Rocco has just left, she decides to go outside to the backyard to lay out in the sun. She's so mad that she talks aloud to herself while lying out.

"This sucks so much! This is freaking the worst summer ever! How did it go from being the best summer to the worst summer? Oh, I know, I just got myself a chronic disease. Nice. Thanks, body. Thanks for betraying me! Did I ask to have this happen to me? Of course not. I'm trying super hard not to say, why me, but it's on the tip of my tongue." She pauses and gazes at the gorgeous blue sky. This is her place of solace, along with her music and drawing. Being outdoors soothes her very soul.

Samantha continues to rant to no one but herself. "Blood checks. Count my carbs and shots and do it all again! There's barely time to do anything because of all I have to do to keep my body going and keep the stupid diabetes maintained. GRRRRRRRR."

She feels a bit better, but she begins to cry before she can stop herself… large, dripping tears. She allows herself to cry and cry and cry. And she lay in the sun and cries, and feels sad, and feels sorry for herself. She feels frustrated and mad, and all of the feels that she could think about this dumb chronic disease, she felt.

She knows it isn't making much sense to blame her body, or to blame anyone in general, but Samantha is angry. She also knows that she can't blame Jules, Rocco, and Bo for hanging together. She's the one who is making the excuses not to be with them all, and though she knows all of this… it still hurts.

Samantha must have laid out in the sun and cried for a couple of hours, but it ends up being very healing for her! She feels like she has purged a lot of feelings that have been bottled up for a good month or so. She feels way better, almost relieved. Who knew a good cry could be so cleansing and therapeutic?

Samantha eventually drags herself into the house and into the kitchen. It's time for a snack before dinner in a couple of hours. Jules had just texted her before Samantha came indoors, asking if she and Bo could come over and say hi! Samantha frowns as she holds her phone and is about to answer when Rocco, Bo, and Jules walk in the front door, chatting and laughing. Samantha freezes. Jules runs over to her and gives her a huge hug! Samantha doesn't reciprocate because she is still in shock!

Bo comes over next. "Samantha! What's up? I feel like I haven't seen you for sooo long! Rocco said you've been dealing with some personal stuff, so Jules and I just were chillin' until you wanted to share stuff with us."

Samantha smiles and pulls out a chair around their large kitchen counter. She smiles at Rocco, too. Her bro, Rocco, has been stellar. He repeatedly asks Samantha to come with them all, but Samantha just can't yet. She's so grateful for her brother—he is literally the bestest—and look how he helps her with Jules and Bo. He's truly a gem.

"Well, I guess we're gonna do this now," Samantha says. "Okay, hey Bo, um, could y'all take a seat? And Jules too. I've got something to share with you."

Everyone pulls out a chair and sits. Samantha gets up, grabs her diabetic go-to bag, and brings it to the countertop.

"Soooo, guys, remember that weekend when our family went on that impromptu trip?"

"Yes," Bo says.

"Well, my mom and I were actually at the Dallas Children's Hospital. It was July 17, and my mom got me a doc appt with our pediatrician at 4:00 P.M. I didn't let anyone know, but I'd been feeling sick to my stomach, chronically thirsty and hungry, and then I had to go to the bathroom all the time during the day and even during the night! It was awful, and I felt awful, and it seemed like the symptoms were getting worse and worse."

She looks at Bo. "Well, unbeknownst to myself and my family, it takes a quick check of your blood glucose to see if you've got a chronic disease, which is what happened to me. I've got a chronic disease called diabetes mellitus, better known as T1D, Type 1 diabetes."

Bo looks surprised, and Samantha keeps talking. "I was in the hospital for three days. I got trained on how to care for myself, which means I learned to calculate the carbohydrates I eat, get a blood check before I eat and two hours after I eat, then I have to give myself a shot of insulin. Apparently, my body destroyed my own insulin-producing cells. It's called an auto-immune disease. Rocco obvi knows, and Jules knows a little bit as she came to visit me in the hospital. Bo, I'm super sorry, but I was too embarrassed to tell you. And Jules, I was too embarrassed to explain it all to you. I was also too embarrassed to have you watch me blood-check myself and give myself shots. I'm sorry, guys. I know we're all friends, but this has been a lot on me." Samantha finishes her spiel with a quiet voice and lowers her head.

Bo, Jules, and Rocco looked toward Samantha. Jules gets up first and goes to hug her. Bo gets up, sits closer to Samantha, and gives her a quick side arm hug around her shoulders. Samantha feels all gooey inside, like a hot and melty chocolate cookie.

"Samantha!" Jules says. "What the heck? I knew you were sick, but I didn't understand exactly why you were in the hospital. I didn't realize just how much you were dealing with all by yourself. I am super sorry. I wish you had told me more, but I don't blame you. I guess I would have been embarrassed, too."

"Seriously, Samantha," Bo says. "I would have been so chill with this cause my uncle Justin has T1D. I think he got diagnosed when he was a teen, like you. He's twenty-eight now and doing so well! He's been on a pump for years now. Can you get an insulin pump?"

"Oh, you guys," Samantha says, tears trickled down her cheeks. "I'm so sorry I didn't include you. I was being stupid and silly, I know, but man! This has been so much! And no way did I want you guys to see me doing blood checks or giving myself shots."

Samantha turns toward Bo to answer his question about the insulin pump. "Yes, but not quite yet. I've got this thing going on called the honeymoon period, which means my pancreas is still producing insulin but sporadically, so it's hard to regulate my doses. But, once I'm out of it, I can get this thing called a CGM—continuous glucose monitor—and then aim for a pump afterward. This could take around eight months to a year, though!"

"Well, that's great news!" Bo smiles at Samantha and takes her hand. Her body feels like it has been electrified from head to toe.

Dang, I like this boy. And we haven't even hung out with each other for over a month, and he's still around. This boy makes me so happy! He's so kind. Why was I so untrusting of him? Oh, I know, because I don't want him to think I'm broken. That's why.

"I am really sorry, you guys!" Samantha tells them. "I should have been more trusting. I'm just so scared to start school. I mean, now I have to go to the nurse to do my blood checks and insulin shots, when all I wanted to do was dress cute and enjoy my classes as an incoming sophomore!"

Everyone laughs! Samantha does too! She wipes her tears and continues to laugh.

"I don't blame you, Samantha! Who wouldn't feel that way?" Jules states in a matter-of-fact way.

"For real, Samantha," Bo says kindly. "Jules and I won't be around when you do blood checks and shots, okay? Will that help?"

The group decides to hang out and talk before dinner time.

Welp! That just happened, but I'm glad it did. Enough slinking around, feeling sorry for myself, and keeping this all to myself. I need support. I need friends. I mean, my family is legit and amazing, but friends are different, and most of all, the boy I am digging into is SUPER important to me!

Dinner time comes before the four of them are ready for it, but being respectful friends, both Bo and Jules head home, and it's yet another mealtime for Samantha, which means a blood check and an insulin shot.

Samantha is getting better at her diabetes management. Shots aren't as big of a deal anymore, blood checks are smoother, and with the apps she can use, even calculating her food isn't so taxing. Today is Thursday, and with school starting the following Monday, she and her mom can go to the high school to meet with the school nurse tomorrow, Friday. By doing this, Samantha won't have to be so flustered on Monday. In Texas, every school has its own nurse—thankfully—otherwise, this diabetes thing would be even more difficult for Samantha.

* * *

On Friday, they have the meet-up with Nurse Melinda Howard —she goes by Nurse Howard—and it goes super well! Samantha feels so much better. Is she still slightly terrified? Absolutely! But apparently, there are a few other diabetic kiddos at the school. While in the clinic, Samantha can load the fridge with string cheese, juice pouches, and her insulin. She even has her own drawer, which she fills with needles and test strips.

Samantha's mom let Nurse Howard know all the calculating info needed for Samantha's carb-to-insulin ratio, gives Nurse Howard her cell, and has a great overall conversation with her. Samantha is reminiscing over this as they're driving home.

"Nurse Howard is so nice! I feel so much better. I'm so glad you were able to set up this appointment, Mom. Thank you."

"Of course, sweetie pea. I knew this would help you. I know I'd want this if I was starting high school and had diabetes."

"Thanks, Mom. I feel at least a little more prepared for Monday. I mean, I still will be THAT KID who has to see the nurse, but at least I can care for myself without people staring at me."

By the time Samantha and her mom get home, Rocco and Bo have finished their shift at the pool—it's actually their last shift—and Jules has popped over, too. After the group chats the previous night, Bo, Jules, Rocco, and Samantha are back as the foursome they had been over a month ago.

They decided to take advantage of the pool tonight and will do the same tomorrow and Sunday. When it's time for a blood check or insulin shot, Samantha will just excuse herself to take care of her diabetes. This will be her new system, and practicing it throughout the weekend is a big plus for Samantha.

It's way better than I thought it could be! I'm grateful everyone is okay with the way I need to care for my diabetes. Phew. What a relief!

14

Sunday Night Before Sophomore Year Starts!

Samantha is lying on her bed musing and mulling over all of the changes that have occurred in her young life since July 17.

Diabetes diagnosis. Fear. Anger. Tears. Then, figuring out how to care for myself with T1D—great support from my family... and now, support from Jules and Bo. School starts tomorrow! Holy crud!! Am I ready? Yeah, I am as ready as I can be! I've got a great and comfortable outfit—sweatshirt included cause In Texas, summer outfits always have a sweatshirt or coat involved since the A/C is so freaking cold! I've got juice pouches and zero soda in my backpack, just in case. My one concern is if I feel low, will I know? And if I am low, can I get to Nurse Howard in time? Ugh. I may need someone to help me, but I will tackle this problem when it happens.

Samantha feels her phone vibrate.

Bo!

Bo: *"Hey Samantha, how are you feeling about school tomorrow? Did you find a 'cute outfit' to wear ha, ha?"*

Samantha: *"Ha, ha, I did indeed! And yes. I was just lying on my bed thinking over the past five weeks or so. A lot has happened. I appreciate you,*

Jules, and Rocco for being so supportive. It's made an enormous difference these past few days for me to not feel so alone in all of this! So well, thanks, is what I'm saying."

Bo: *"No need for thanks. That's what friends do for each other. K, see ya tomorrow!"*

Samantha: *"See ya! Thanks for the text!"*

Friends? Friends? Okay, Samantha, chill out, of course, you're just friends. Have you held hands? NO. Have you kissed? NO. Now, do I WANT to be more than friends? Uh, heck, yes, and I hope we eventually become more than just friends sooner than later, but alas, I must wait to date cause in my family, we have a rule that we don't date until we turn sixteen, which for me is in December. It's our family rule, and I'm cool with this. Luckily, I am not pressured to date or hang out with Bo exclusively. Not gonna lie; the thought surely crossed my mind when I looked into that boy's beautiful face and dreamy dark eyes. But, truly, and in all honesty, I have too much on my plate to think about anyone's emotional well-being except my own, so friends we shall be!

Samantha slips into her bed, ready to draw and listen to music before falling asleep, when she hears a soft knock on her door.

"Come in!"

It's Rocco. He peeks around my door. "Hey, sis, how are you doing?"

"Good! I feel okay. I feel pretty good. Bo just texted me."

"Ah, no wonder you're so happy!"

"Okay, please...." Samantha laughs.

"I should ask how the heck you are. Are you ready? Junior year!"

"Yeah. No biggie for me. I like our high school. I've got a decent schedule, so I'm good. And I am liking Jules.

"It's been a good summer with us all hanging together, that's for sure."

"It really has," she agrees. "Bo is a great friend."

"Well, I'm glad you feel ready for school."

"Oh!" she adds. "The only thing I stress about is getting low blood sugar and not being able to walk to Nurse Howard's office, like, do I have someone help me?"

"Oh, that's a reality for sure. Didn't even think about this. I guess this week, maybe find some allies in your classes? Talk with Mom and Nurse Howard?"

"Yeah, good idea! K, I gotta get some sleep, bro. Scoot! Out you go!"

"Okay, okay, and oh! Be ready by 8:10 A.M.

"Yes sir! Just kidding, love you, Rocco."

15

First Day of Sophomore Year
(Now, as a T1 diabetic/T1D!)

The first day of school has come!

Samantha rises earlier than usual, dresses, and applies simple makeup—eye shadow and lip gloss—as her face is still very tan. Her coloring is already a lovely olive green, so even when she isn't tan, she doesn't wear very much because she doesn't need it. *Thankfully!*

Her biggest fear about starting school today is how much her lifestyle change will affect her. At home, at least, she can handle everything comfortably, with her family helping and supporting her.

I am not looking forward to this part of starting my sophomore year today! It's already stressful enough to be still considered one of the little fish at high school, let alone starting your second year with a newly diagnosed freaking chronic disease!!

Samantha had been feeling better emotionally about her T1D overall, but right now, she feels so anxious! She continues to get ready, but an entourage of what-ifs and other questions flooded her brain.

Can I keep my diabetes lifestyle to myself? What if others in class or the nurse's office ask me questions? What if I get a low blood sugar and have to pump-up in a class? What if I get really low? What if I get really high? What if people see me eating my snacks or drinking my juice pouch? AARRGGHH! Too many questions! I'm just gonna have to suck it up and get out the door to what ifs will happen today... no choice.

Samantha had packed her newly purchased backpack over the weekend. Fortunately, she'd found a stellar JanSport backpack with enough pockets to hold her supplies: her blood checker, fifteen-carb snacks, three juice pouches, and her glucagon kit, which is for emergencies when she's too low. She can bring all these items to class with her, but Samantha can NOT blood check in class nor give herself shots in class. She is required to see Nurse Howard, who, in turn, will keep documentation of all the carbs of the food Samantha eats, plus her blood glucose numbers and the amount of insulin she injects. Samantha must also eat snacks in certain classes or drink a juice pouch. Samantha has a doctor's note, but not all teachers will know. She'll need to show the note before every dang class, and Samantha also has a note from her mother. Her mom will email every teacher after she goes to school today.

"CRAP! It's almost 7:50 A.M. I need to eat before I go to school! I am so nervous. I feel nauseous." Samantha's talking to herself as she packs up the rest of her daily needs.

Samantha races down the stairs, flies into the kitchen, and grabs a banana and a packet of oatmeal.

"Good morning, precious. Are you as ready as you can be for today?"

"Sure, Mom, feeling GREAT!" Samantha gives her mom a very stressed look, which is apparent in the tone of her answer.

"Darlin', you CAN do this. And if you need anything, I will come up, okay? Also, any time you're in Nurse Howard's office, you can call or text Dad or me, okay? I know this is a lot. I wish you didn't have to deal with this, sweetie, more than anything, but I believe YOU ARE SO BRAVE, Samantha Kate. So brave. I know I couldn't do half of what you've had to do so far to maintain your diabetes."

Samantha sees tears start to well up in her mom's eyes. She walks over to her mom, who hugs her tightly.

Samantha inhales her mother's scent, then pulls back. "I know I can, Mom, it's just… a lot, and there are many uncertainties."

Her mom agrees and pours in hot water for Samantha's oatmeal. She stirs it and adds a small amount of milk, and Samantha scarfs down her food. Then, she grabs a needle, pulls up her insulin into the needle from the insulin vial, flicks it with her fingers to get out any air bubbles, and gives herself a shot in her upper arm.

"Lunchtime will be tough," she tells her mom. "I don't know how to rush the blood check, calculate, give insulin, or process any faster."

"Yes, I agree. The unknowns are going to be tough obstacles to work through. This phrase may be trite, but daily, darlin', day by day."

"Yeah, Dr. Swaneyard always says that to me." Samantha finishes packing her lunch and puts it into her backpack.

Earlier this morning, Samantha had checked her blood glucose level. Her result was 135, within the normal range for a T1D. Although the normal range is 80-120 for non-diabetics, people with T1D have a different sliding scale. Newly diagnosed people need to adjust very well to their disease, and if they can keep it in control for a long time, they can aim for a more normal range.

Samantha checks and rechecks her backpack.

Thankfully, I can bring these items and thankfully, I can blood check and give shots in the nurse's office since I have zero intention of making this chronic disease of mine public until I get a CGM and an insulin pump. ABSOLUTELY PRIVATE!

"Let's go, Samantha!" her brother calls.

"Ready!"

"Bye, my beauties! Best of luck to you both today!" Her mom waves and smiles after Rocco and Samantha take off in a slight sprint to get to the Honda.

While driving to school, Samantha texts Jules to ask her to save her a spot in the large cafeteria where the sophomores and freshmen eat.

Jules: *"Of course! See you at school!"*

Samantha: *"Thank u"*

They park, and Rocco waves goodbye to Samantha as they split up and enter their different hallways.

"See you sis! Hang in there, okay?"

"Thanks, Rocco. I will do my best!"

She waves back to Rocco. Samantha walks rapidly to D Hall to find her first-period classroom. Luckily, she had already walked through her full class schedule when meeting Nurse Howard. Samantha found her class and went in.

And my day has begun!

Samantha was grateful she had made it through periods one and two. She also recognized quite a few friends from her freshman year in both classes, which was a plus for her. It made her feel more acclimated despite her diabetes-care fears.

So far so good! Now, my third class of the day. Phew! Then, lunch!

By the end of the third period, though, Samantha is feeling "low"— a sensation where you live your life and do everyday activities, and then, wham! You feel like you have not eaten for days. She sneakily pulls out a juice and downs it at her desk. Right now, Samantha decided not to check her blood glucose because she knows that lunch is coming up, and she is starting to feel more and more when she gets a low blood sugar. She does not do this often because it's not very smart, but she does it today since she already has a stress case inside her.

Luckily, no one notices the juice pouch—or so she thinks.

DANG IT.

But Samantha's teacher did see her, and he motions for her to approach his desk. Samantha slowly gets up, hoping no one is watching her. Luckily, everyone is very engaged during their individual reading time. Samantha, unfortunately, wasn't able to show Mr. Johnson her notes before class started, but instead had to find a desk upon arrival, so that sucks, and now she is being called to the front. She still feels woozy but manages to get up and walk to him.

"Samantha, why are you drinking a juice pouch in class? Do you not know the school rules? No food or drink in class. Period," Mr. Johnson says.

Without saying anything, Samantha produces two notes from her pocket: one from Doctor Swaneyard and one from her mother. Mr. Johnson read the notes, muttering something under his breath, and says, "Fine."

That was it. Not anything else, such as, "Gee, Samantha, I am sorry, are you okay?" Just an abrupt "fine" and a sweeping gesture for her to return to her desk.

I can't wait for lunchtime. Ughhhh. This is so stressful!!

The bell rings, and Samantha gets up as quickly as possible and high-tails it to Nurse Howard.

"Welcome in, Samantha! Let the fun begin!"

Samantha smiles as she hears Nurse Howard's greeting. "How has it gone so far, sweetie?"

"Well, other than when Mr. Johnson called me up to ask me why I was drinking a juice pouch, and also the fact that he didn't even care one bit WHY I was drinking a juice Pouch, everything has been good! I've been pretty stressed, though, not gonna lie!"

"Of course you are! This new lifestyle is still so new, and I'm sure you've got a lot going on in that cute brain of yours. I consider that a win with Mr. Johnson because he can be difficult to deal with. We will take what we get for now. Come on over, Samantha, and let's get you set to eat your lunch."

Samantha smiles and nods in agreement with Nurse Howard's request. Then, she takes out her blood glucose monitor and checks her glucose level.

89

"Okay. Thanks. I'll record that. Now, let's count your carbs and give you some Humalog (fast-acting insulin).

"Oh, look! Aww, my mom is so sweet! She's calculated the carbs for me already."

"Awesome, that was so sweet of her. I really liked your mom. I am always glad to meet supportive and loving parents. Okey, dokey, now, if you can get your insulin ready and give yourself a shot, then you can go to the large cafeteria to eat with all the other sophomores."

Samantha did just that… got her insulin out, filled her needle, gave herself her shot, and shoved half of her sandwich into her mouth as she left the nurse's office and walked toward the larger cafeteria. While walking, she texted Jules.

Samantha: *"Heading to the cafeteria. Have a spot for me?"*

Jules didn't answer immediately, which was weird. Then, she finally answered.

Jules: *"Sure"*

Sure? What's with the one-word answer, Jules? And what the heck does that mean? Like, is it a chore for my bestie to save a spot for me? I texted her this morning to see if she could save me a spot, and she was more than happy to do so. What changed?

Samantha finishes the other half of her sandwich and walks into the cafeteria. She begins scanning the tables for Jules.

Holy crap! There are a lot of people!

Samantha continues to look around in the hopes of seeing Jules.

Finally!

Samantha spots her. Thankfully. Samantha then sees who Jules is sitting with.

Ugh. Why is Jules sitting with Melody? She's so rude to Jules—every time. Well, actually, she's rude to everyone! Gladly, I can manage to ignore her rudeness and will absolutely not play into her stupid, mean-girl crap.

"Hey everyone!" Samantha smiles as she approaches the table of people. She can scoot next to Jules, but it's a tight squeeze. Melody is sitting on Jules's other side.

"Oh, hi, Samantha! Glad you could join us!" Melody says sarcastically to Samantha. Samantha doesn't skip a beat and comes right back with an answer. "Oh, my gosh, you're soooo welcome. Thanks so much for saving me a spot, Jules and Melody. Had to use the restroom before lunch." Samantha says confidently, giving Melody a smirk, and then turns abruptly away from Melody to talk to Jules.

"How were your first three periods, Jules?" Samantha asks sweetly.

"Good! I found all my classes, and I like my teachers. Thankfully. Ha, ha."

"Right? Me too. I am so relieved we made it to this point in our day. I mean, I know we came last year, but having classes in different wings this year makes a difference."

"For real! I was worried I'd not make it for the third period. I was almost late!"

"Oh, dang, sorry, Jules. It's a little stressful, sheesh!"

They continue to chat, and Samantha eats the rest of her lunch before the bell rings to make everyone aware that it's time to get to their next class. Luckily, Melody left them alone and spent the entire lunch period talking to her best friend, Hannah.

They're both pretty into themselves. I hope to avoid them as much as possible this year. Especially Melody. She's a real piece of work.

Unbeknownst to anyone else, Samantha carefully ate everything in her lunch. No way did she want to have another low blood sugar if she could avoid it, which could happen… nonetheless, Samantha was committed to doing her part as best as possible!

Jules and Samantha hustle to clean up and get on their way. Since the high school does not have lockers, they have to take their backpacks everywhere, which is a crazy concept. They did it last year, but it's still just as dumb this year, and here they are, reliving this reality once more.

I'm not *sure who came up with that genius idea, but boy, is it a pain to carry our backpacks all day! There may be a budget down the road to remedy this and build us some lockers. My back is going to be wrecked!*

Samantha and Jules parted ways, each walking quickly to their respective classes. They have one class together, advanced Spanish, in sixth period, so it's nice to have the same class and be able to reconnect each day.

"See ya later, Jules!"

"Kk, see you in sixth period, Samantha!"

16

Samantha thinks to herself as she rapidly walks to class. She is very glad that Jules seemed her regular self at lunch after her weird one-word response, "sure."

I still don't know why Jules was sitting with Melody! The girl drives me nuts. I sure hope Melody won't influence Jules at all with her meanness. Ugh. She's so bossy and snotty. And rude!

Thankfully, fourth and fifth periods pass without any incidents for Samantha, for which she is most grateful!

Hallelujah!!

"Hola, Chiquita!" Jules says as Samantha enters their shared classroom.

"Hola, amiga!" Samantha responds.

Samantha and Jules laugh, knowing they are Espanol dorks. But at least they're Spanish dorks together. They both wander around to decide which spots to snatch so they can sit by each other. They pick a table that is two tables back from the front of the classroom. Samantha unpacks her five-subject spiral, grabs a pen, and sits down. There are two other girls already sitting, and both Jules and Samantha give them a wave. Then, the four of them exchange pleasantries and ask each other a few questions. It turns out that both of the girls were in Spanish 2 class last year, too.

"Hola, todos!"

Samantha and Jules straighten themselves to face the front.

Everyone responds to the teacher with a, "Hola, signora!"

Samantha had already been very excited about this class. She loves Spanish, and she and Jules passed their Spanish 2 class with flying colors in ninth grade. So, this accelerated class will be fabulous for them both. Ms. Alba takes them through the semester syllabus and her class expectations, and then the period is over.

"One more period! Bye, Jules!"

"Bye, Samantha. I'll text you after school."

"Sounds good!

Seventh period starts pretty well, but then Samantha suddenly starts to feel woozy. Samantha knows that still being in her "honeymoon period" tends to make for a lot of low blood glucose levels.

Oh no! Not again. This is why the honeymoon period is such a pain. Because who knows when extra insulin is gonna squirt out?

Samantha raises her hand to ask to use the restroom because if she can go into the bathroom, she can use the blood test kit in her backpack to perform a blood test and drink a juice. She gets approval from the teacher to go, so she hurriedly grabs her blood test kit and a juice pouch and locks herself into a stall. Samantha checks her glucose and sure enough, she is.

56. No wonder I feel so crappy!

She downs two juice pouches and then sits on the closed toilet for about five more minutes. She's finally feeling better, so she grabs her trash, chucks it out, has her blood checker in her hand, grabs the bathroom pass, and returns to her art class. Everyone is busy working on a get-to-know-you scavenger hunt, so she slips into the classroom and grabs her paper, pretending she hadn't been in the bathroom for fifteen minutes.

I do need to talk to my mom and Nurse Howard about when I have a low. There has got to be a better way. But if I can obtain permission from the teachers to go to the bathroom, then no one can see me blood-check, and then

I won't have to go down to Nurse Howard's office. Yeah, I know it's not the nurse's office, but I'll deal with that later. This may be the only way to do it from here on out.

She will most likely need to discuss the low blood sugar situation with Nurse Howard and her mom. It was while she was in the restroom that she realized that she hadn't even heard from Bo for the entire day. Samantha knows he's in no way obligated to text her throughout the day, but she also thinks it would be great to hear from him and see how his first day has gone.

Okay, chill out, Samantha. I need to remember we're just friends. Even if we both dig each other, well, I dig him and hope he digs me, but for now, we're just friends. Should I even text him later? Okay, well, if I'm just being a friend, then yes, I can text him after school and ask how his day went, right? And share about my day? That would be okay, I think. I'll see how I feel about all this when I get home.

Samantha and her classmates finish the scavenger hunt. She actually enjoyed it and made a couple of new friends. Returning to her seat, she glances behind her and sees Bo!

How did I not see him? I sat down, then started to feel low, and left. Yeah, that makes sense. Art is an elective class that only sophomores and AP students can take. I didn't know that he liked art. I love art. I'm hoping to improve this year, and now that I've been diagnosed with diabetes, I think I need to use my art to channel my emotions.

Samantha figures Bo was sitting way behind her. And class had just started when she'd gone to the restroom.

Anyway, he sees her now and waves. She waves back. They have another ten minutes before the bell rings to end the day. They're in groups, depending on how many similar answers they got that matched other class members.

I guess Bo and I hadn't really talked about his schedule. Just maybe her schedule. Great, now I'm not even a good friend! I need to be more attentive to asking Bo questions and finding out about him, not just have my diabetes, lifestyle change, take over my entire existence.

She and the other three students in her group continued to chat about this upcoming art elective.

Should I wait for Bo outside the classroom? Should I just pretend to walk slowly? Who knows? These situations seriously make me so nervous! What's the correct answer to this question, and is there a protocol? Cause if there is, I surely don't know it!!

The bell rings, and she's getting up and packing her stuff up when Bo comes right up to her. She looks up into his beautiful hazel-green eyes.

Dreamy—so dreamy, and thank goodness he came up to me. I was gonna feel seriously awkward.

"Samantha!! How did we not even see each other?" Bo laughs heartily.

"I've no idea! I did have to use the restroom right as class started, and I think y'all were deep into the scavenger hunt."

"Sure, that makes sense. Anyway, it's cool that we are having class together." Bo smiles, and Samantha feels slightly weak in her knees— and no, it's not a low blood sugar!

"Is Rocco taking you home, I suppose?"

"Yeah, I'm lucky cause I've got an older brother with a car."

"Sure are! But, Samantha…" Bo says, staring right into Samantha's eyes. She's legit mesmerized with his dark skin, dark hair, and dreamy eyes. "I'm really glad we've got a class together."

Samantha gains her bearings. "Oh! Me too, and Bo, I'm sorry I didn't ask you about your schedule. That's not being a very good friend. I'm sorry."

"Uh, no worries at all cause I just snagged this class today. Had to shuffle some of my classes around anyway. So, hey, I'm gonna head home. I'll text ya later?"

"That would be fantastic, sure! Bye!"

Wow. Did I sound a little too eager? Or over joyous? Hopefully, Bo didn't sense my ecstatic joy at having him in art class. Did he? Cause, dang, that boy is the sweetest and so freaking gorgeous. I'm so preoccupied with my dang diabetes that I have forgotten how adorable he is. Well, he is more gorgeously adorable! Is that even a word?

Samantha giggles to herself as she packs up. If she had speech bubbles following her around all day, like in a graphic novel, the other students would def think she's slightly crazy!!

Samantha's phone vibrates.

Rocco: *"Yo, sis, where the heck are you?"*

Samantha: *"Sorry! Almost to the car."*

Samantha all but jogs to the Honda and sees her brother's adorable face and smile, which warms her heart. She always feels safe with him around her. She opens the passenger side door. Rocco is already seated, with the car on, and has his seatbelt on. He means business when it comes to leaving school, apparently!

"Hey! Sorry. Still getting used to carrying ninety pounds around with me!" Samantha happily laughs.

"For real. Welcome to the "no-locker" club."

Rocco pulls out, and they exchange information about their first day of the school year. "How was the diabetes maintenance?"

"Not too bad for day one. I need to iron out a few wrinkles, like when I feel low. Do I hide in the bathroom? Do I go to Nurse Howard? That kind of stuff. How will your classes be this semester?"

"Hard, busy, but good. Can't complain... as of yet," Rocco gives Samantha his signature smirk.

"Good thing you're like a brainiac!"

"I don't know about that, but you know I don't mind school."

"Yeah, me neither. I feel okay about all of my teachers so far. I mean, it's only day one!" Samantha laughs.

Rocco pulls the Honda to the curb, and they grab their stuff and pile it out. Their mom should be home soon, so they can tell her all the details of our day before she heads out to get Janey from elementary school.

* * *

After dinner, Samantha is in her room sorting through her syllabuses and using her planning book to write down assignments when she feels her phone vibrate.

Bo: *"Hey Samantha, what did you decide to do for your self-portrait project?"*

BO! Her stomach flutters.

Act casual! Right! I may explode whenever I see him, let alone when I get a text from him. Geez.

Samantha: *"Hey back, I think I will draw myself in my favorite color, purple, and then use the words to describe me as an option, you?"*

Bo: *"Cool idea. Well, since I am the least artistic human ever, I will use the words option too. I like using your favorite color. Maybe I'll do the same. Are you cool if I copy your idea?"*

Samantha: *"Of course! I've been sorting through my syllabus for what feels like hours, writing everything in my planner. Dang it's a lot!"*

Bo: *"Ahhh, and don't we just loveee high school?"*

Samantha: *"Yeah! I forgot how much busy work type stuff we have to do this first week."*

Bo*: "It will chill out a bit, but I never like how they swamp you with everything right in the first week or two until the classes get into a routine with homework, tests, etc."*

Samantha: *"For realz"*

Bo*: "I forgot to ask how your diabetes stuff went today."*

Samantha: *"Yeah, not too bad. I had two lows, hid out in the bathroom for one, then got busted in class for the other, so gotta work out those kinks."*

Bo: *"Ha, sorry! But wow, good job. It must be weird to have to care for yourself in this way now, I'm assuming?"*

She nods. **Samantha**: *"Very weird. I'm trying hard to keep it very private until I get a CGM and a pump. Those things will make my diabetes care way more discreet, ya know."*

Bo: *"Yeah, I do. My uncle Justin will be in town in October, speaking of, so I hope we can coordinate for you to meet him"*

Samantha: *"I would love that"*

Bo: *"Gotta go-Claire is bugging me to play a game with her. Brother duty calls. See ya in art class"*

Samantha: *"See ya. Thanks for texting me."*

Samantha had just ended that thread with Bo only to start another thread with Jules. **Samantha**: *"Are you getting organized?"*

Jules: *"Trying to! Sheesh, it is taking me forever. Plus everyone over here is acting like a wild animal. You'd think going to school all day would wear them out, but apparently not"*

Samantha: *"Sorry, I hope you get it all done. I'm making some progress, but yeah, it's taking forever. Hey, sorry about being late for lunch. It's gonna be that way until I get a pump, so…"*

Jules: *"Not a problem. See you tomorrow at lunch."*

Samantha: *"Kk, bye"*

Samantha does one last blood check before bed, eats a bedtime snack, and then gives herself slow-acting insulin. This insulin will carry her through the night hours. When she gets a pump, goodbye shots, and hello button pushing because it will also have a continuous insulin drip to mimic the pancreas.

I'm sure I need to feel some gratitude in my world somewhere for all of this diabetes stuff. As Nurse Beth taught us, having shots and insulin is amazing, even since its discovery in 1921. I mean, it's only 2025! Over 100 years is all. But how can I even think of that when I'm just trying to make it to my next blood check or snack?

17

SAMANTHA RELOADS her juice pouches and checks her vial of test strips. She also loads up a few more snacks. At least she can eat those while walking between classes, and for fifteen-carb snacks, she doesn't need a shot.

She'd also had a good discussion with her mom about her low blood sugar episodes and what to do. Mom emailed all of Samantha's teachers explaining about her diabetes and how if she is feeling the least bit poorly, Samantha would need to see Nurse Howard. Her mom was very clear that Samantha would need accommodations for this and would be leaving third period early to do a blood check and give herself an insulin shot before lunchtime. She copied the house principal and the counselor on every email to ensure they give Samantha the time she needs to care for herself.

Samantha feels a bit like a slacker and doesn't want any special treatment, but until she gets the CGM and then the insulin pump after that, she has no other options but to go to the nurse's office for her shots and blood checks, and now pump-ups. Her mom asked that any work Samantha may miss be added to Samantha's homework if needed.

Samantha knows this will be a lot until she gets that CGM, hopefully by the end of October.

Ready for school and ready for bed, Samantha crawls into her delightful, comfy queen bed. She turns out her light but stares at the ceiling for a long while, thinking and thinking before nodding off to sleep. There is much to ponder.

I hope I can handle this diabetes stuff day in and day out while doing classwork and homework, maintaining friendships, and hopefully becoming more than just friends with Bo....

* * *

THE DAYS CRUISE BY FOR SAMANTHA THAT FIRST WEEK OF SCHOOL. BY day five, Friday, Samantha feels a weird twinge of frustration from Jules during lunch.

"Where have you been, Samantha? I can only hold your spot for so long," Jules says, irritated.

"I'm sorry, Jules. I can do nothing about it until I get that CGM device. And by the way, why are we sitting with Melody and Hannah every day?"

"Why not? What's wrong with Melody and Hannah?"

"What's wrong is cause Melody is a jerk, and Hannah does whatever Melody wants, and if you hadn't noticed, Melody is anything but nice to you."

"She's nice to me," Jules says with apparent hesitation. "Plus we're in a lot of classes together, and she's popular!" Jules whispered this last part in Samantha's ear.

Samantha rolls her eyes and sits down. This time, she sits by Melody to protect and shield Jules.

"Samantha," Melody begins, "Why is it taking so long for you to come to lunch every day? I mean, I can't keep saving a seat for you. Many, many people want to sit with us."

"Well, gosh, thanks then for saving a spot for me. But actually, it's been Jules who's been saving my spot, so you don't even have to worry your pretty little head about me one more minute!" Samantha oozes this out with a sort of sweet sarcasm.

Melody harrumphs and turns to talk Hannah's ear off.

Good! Leave me and my Jules friend alone already!

By week two, Samantha's teachers were much more cooperative and compliant. This change was only possible because Nurse Howard had to use legal jargon in an email to them. She had to reiterate that blood checks, shots, pump-ups, and treating high blood sugar are done in her office!

"These teachers think you kids with diabetes are just trying to get out of class," Nurse Howard tells her. "Honestly! I have to do this at the beginning of each new school year! You'd think they'd learn by now, but no! I've got to be the bad guy! It gets old."

Samantha smiles and says, "Well, I, for one, thank you for your help. This week has been much better."

"Okay, that's good to hear," the nurse says. "And remember, don't hesitate one bit to tell me if a teacher is uncooperative."

"Yes, ma'am!"

Samantha had been in the nurse's office with a low blood sugar just as she was going to sixth period. She felt much better as she drank her juice pouch, rested for about ten minutes, and then did a blood check again to make sure she is pumped up enough. *143.*

Samantha can go back to sixth period. She had at least thirty minutes left in Spanish. Hopefully, the class has not done too much while she was absent. Samantha walks into class quietly and quickly sits in her seat.

"Where have you been?" Jules says to Samantha, sounding annoyed.

"Low blood sugar—geez," Samantha says this with just as much annoyance. Samantha has to gather herself before asking Jules her next question. "What are we doing right now?" Samantha softens her tone a bit.

"On Canvas, we will read and answer questions, and then we will do partner discussions," Jules says crisply.

"Thanks." Samantha does *not* like Jules's impatience or this discussion one bit. She can barely concentrate the entire time she attempts to complete her assignment! Her mind isn't calm at all!

WHY is Jules bugged with ME? DID I ask to get diabetes? Uhhhh, heck no. Did I ask to get a low blood sugar? NO. Geez. I don't know what this annoyance is all about, but I don't need it!

It was partner discussion time. Signora Alba asked the class to switch from their table mates and pick different partners.

GLADLY.

Samantha walks toward Peter. He's a friendly kid. She's known him for a few years. He consents to partner with her, and they have a great discussion. Peter has an abuela (a grandmother) who lives in Mexico, so he's well versed in Espanol but has to take a language for high school credits. Class is almost over, so everyone starts to pack up. Samantha is ready to go right as the bell rings.

"See ya, Jules," Samantha says without really looking her way or letting Jules even answer. WHY is this bothering Samantha so much? She's not sure, but it is.

Art is not her favorite class today because they couldn't sit where they wanted to.

Sigh.

But Samantha finishes her classwork, packs up, and heads for the door because she knows Rocco will text her any minute if she is not in the car. In class, she and Bo didn't even get to visit today!

GRRR! This day HAS NOT ended well! Gosh dang it.

Fortunately, as Samantha is packing up, she catches Bo's line of sight and waves. He smiles and waves back. He then holds up his phone and points to it. Samantha gives him a thumbs-up with her free hand. Then, she scurries out of the classroom to meet Rocco at his car.

Son of a biscuit! At least I got to smile and wave to Bo, but holy. Jules has made me beyond angry.

Samantha opens her door with anger and shuts it with even more anger.

"Woah, woah. What is happening?"

"Jules is happening," she says.

"Jules, Jules?"

"Yes, duh. Which other Jules do I know?"

"Okay, well, when you're feeling less murderous, want to tell me what happened?"

Samantha gives Rocco the most sarcastic thumbs-up ever.

"Oh, boy," Rocco breathes out.

Samantha takes the entire drive home to chill out. As they round the corner to their cul-de-sac, she begins to speak. "I mean, please. It's not like I asked to get diabetes, right?"

Rocco opens his mouth to talk, but Samantha cuts him off before he even starts.

"Well, I didn't. It's not my fault when I get a low blood sugar. Jules acted so put out that I was late to class. Well, sorry, Jules, but I'm not allowed to do a blood check in the classroom. Duh. She knows this by now. She was sooo curt with me. It was absurd."

Rocco, being a very intelligent boy and having lived with three girls his whole life, responded with these words. "Well, that sucks. I'm sorry."

"Thank you, Rocco. I'm done talking about this. Let's go."

As the night wears on, Samantha has to tell her parents her tale of Jules two more times. She's helping with dinner prep when she feels her phone vibrate.

Better be Jules with an apology.

But it sure wasn't. It was Bo, though, who helped lighten her spirits.

Bo: *"Hey you, did you guys eat yet?"*

Samantha: *"Just finishing dinner prep now. What's up?"*

Bo: *"Wondering if you'd like to see a movie Saturday. Well, tomorrow night, but, um, like, just you and me?"*

Samantha stares at her phone, slightly stunned.

Holy cannoli! Is he asking me out OUT?

Samantha: *"That sounds great. Let me check with my parents. I'll text ya later tonight"*

Bo: *"Cool"*

Cool, but NOT COOL cause we've got that family rule, and I'm not 16 until December 18! So, I know what my parents will say!

Dinner is done. Samantha has been working on her homework for a couple of hours when her mom knocks on her door.

"Come in!" Samantha yells.

"Hey, kiddo, how's it going?"

"Good. Just finishing up one more assignment before I get ready for bed."

"Well done. So, this thing with Jules will probably blow over, huh? High school can be complicated, as you're rapidly figuring it out."

"Very."

"Okay, yes, so I'm saying don't give up on her yet. You two have been fast friends for well over four years now."

"I am well aware of this, Mom, but she's the one who had an attitude with me, and for what? Because I was late coming to class cause I had low blood sugar? That's hateful."

"True, very unkind and not at all cool. Anyway, I just wanted to share that with you."

Samantha's facial features soften a bit. "Yeah, okay, I'll take it under advisement."

"Good!"

"Oh, Mom, um… before I forget, Bo asked me to go to the movies with him on Saturday night. Can I go?"

"Just you two?"

"Uh, yeah, I mean, I'm almost sixteen."

"Sure, yep, you sure are, but what happened to the foursome?"

"I don't know. Bo just asked if I wanted to go."

"Let me just run it by Dad. You guys are still just keeping it as friendship, right?"

"Yeah, we sure are. Just friends." Samantha smiles to herself.

But he's the most attractive friend that I sure hope turns into us dating at some point.

"K, I'll let you know in just a bit."

"K, thanks."

Samantha finishes her assignment, brushes her teeth, doodles while listening to some lo-fi tunes, and thinks about things.

Why aren't we going as a foursome? I'll ask Rocco on the way to school tomorrow. Maybe he'll know. And I bet anything that Melody is the one who's talking crap to Jules about me. She makes my blood boil!

Her phone vibrates, and this time it's her mom from the other room.

Mom: *"We'd still rather you went with Bo as a group, if possible. I know that's awkward to tell him, but I'm hoping he'll understand."*

Samantha: *"Sure. Thanks. Night."*

Samantha figured as much since she knew the family rule, but she hadn't wanted to tell Bo quite yet.

Add this on top of my partly crappy day, and voila! I'm feeling just great!

Samantha turns out her light and goes to bed. She'd done all of her diabetes care after she'd done some drawing.

Goodnight, Jules. Thanks for being a jerk. Get ready, Bo, for my family rule. Friday should be peachy.

18

AND PEACHY IT surely is not. In fact, Samantha wakes up around 6:00 A.M. feeling very low. She texts her mom to come and help her. She was 48!

Samantha's mom comes rushing in. "Sorry, sweetie! Let's drink two juice pouches, and then I guess we're up for the day!"

"Yep!" Samantha can't even be sassy because her head hurts. Badly.

"Looking forward to getting my CGM and having this blasted honeymoon period over. I wish it could be now!"

Samantha's mom gives her a big hug and kisses her cheek. "I know, my precious. Me too."

Samantha dresses, eats, gives herself a shot, and runs out the door. Fridays have always been her favorite day of the week, and she sincerely hopes this will never change.

Samantha floats through her day, trying not to think too hard about Jules, her diabetes, and Bo. This concept is virtually impossible since those things are the focus of her life right now.

Lunchtime. Oh, goody.

As she has every day for two weeks, Samantha walks into the swarming beehive of the student cafeteria and looks around for Jules.

She sees her and walks toward the table, only to see that there is definitely NOT a spot for her.

Okay. Play it cool.

"Hey, everyone, sorry I'm late, I was—"

To Samantha's utter surprise, Melody snot-head cuts her off and says in such a terribly mean way, "Oh, we know why you were late, Samantha, and why you've been late every single day since school started."

Samantha opens her eyes widely. She probably looks like she has saucers for eyes. "Umm, what?" This phrase is all that Samantha can eke out.

Melody gets up and comes close to where she is almost in Samantha's face. "It's cause you've got some weird sugar-blood disease, isn't it?"

Samantha freezes. She looks at Jules, who looks horrified. Then, Samantha turns back to Melody, ready to tell her off. "That is none of your business, Melody. And whoever told you that doesn't know what they're talking about!"

Samantha spins around and walks away. She just keeps walking and ends up back at the nurse's office. Tears are threatening to spill out of her eyeballs at any moment.

I trusted you, Jules. I trusted you with a very important and personal secret.

Nurse Howard looks at Samantha's face and pulls her into a hug. Samantha accepts the hug and returns to sit and finish her lunch.

"You are welcome here anytime for lunch. And you can talk if you'd like… or not. Whatever you're comfortable with, okay?"

Samantha nods in the affirmative but doesn't dare speak for fear of becoming a blubbering baby. She just sits quietly, finishes her lunch, packs up, and waits for the bell to ring.

"Oh no! We have Spanish together in sixth period!" Samantha says aloud as she approaches the door.

"Whatever is going on, you can handle it," the nurse says. "I see how invested you've been in your diabetes management. Stand tall. Be strong. Blow off, haters."

Samantha smiles at Nurse Howard and walks out the door.

Nurse Howard is right. Forget it. I will not let Melody or Jules bring me down. Nope. No way, no how.

Samantha does just that. She chooses to be nice and friendly to Jules, pretending that her heart hasn't been crushed during lunch today and that Jules hasn't wholly betrayed her. Samantha could see that Jules is shocked by her happy-go-lucky behavior, but she feigned that she doesn't care.

She makes it through sixth period and is so happy to go to Art, except for the talk she will have with Bo. Samantha exhales a very long sigh as she turns down the hallway.

What is my life right now? For real!!

Samantha rolls her eyes at herself and her life and enters the class with a lot of fake-it-till-she-makes-it confidence. And then she sees Bo.

Heart melt. Oh, and he's wearing that purple and blue shirt. Dang. So gorgeous. Okay, I need to focus and not let my heart override my sensibility. HAH! Right!

Samantha takes her seat. Today, they will share their personality portraits and explain why they chose their colors, words, etc. This activity will take at least three class periods, which is good because she won't have to talk to anyone. As for Bo, she'll speak with him after class. Hopefully, it will go well.

RRIINNGGG

Goodbye! The weekend is here! Hallelujah!!

Samantha is packing up.

"Hi, Samantha, how's it going?"

"Hey, Bo, good, yeah. You?"

"Yeah, all good. I liked hearing everyone's explanation of the personal portraits that they shared today. Did you?"

"Oh, I just loved it! I'm super glad I chose Art as my elective! I am making myself draw more at home, too."

"That's so cool! Good for you. Uh, so any word about Saturday?"

CRAPPITY CRAP!

"I figured my parents would say as much, but we have a rule in our family that we do group dates until we're sixteen, so you and I going alone together is a no. I'm sorry if that's frustrating to you. My birthday is December 18, and I'll be sixteen then. I should have just been up front with you the other night. I choose to follow this family rule, but I'm not naive enough to think you'll stay and continue hanging with me. And that's okay!" Samantha feels her phone vibrate. Rocco. "I'm sorry, I gotta go, Bo. Rocco is chomping at the bit!"

"Yeah, sure, of course. K. Um, I'll check in with you later, okay?"

Samantha smiles at him, slowly shimmies by the other students in her way, and cruises out of the classroom. She saunters more, then walks to Rocco's car.

Welp, that's over. Cool. Nice knowing you, most gorgeous and sweet boy!

Samantha opens her passenger door and gives Rocco the craziest face!

"That good, eh?"

"You've no idea! Take us home, Jeeves!"

They look at each other and laugh, and Rocco takes that as a sign to put on some rockin' tunes and turn it way up high!

* * *

CGM

LET'S DO A QUICK RECAP TO THIS POINT. IT'S NOW OCTOBER. Samantha has eaten lunch with Nurse Howard since THAT DAY. She loves her classes... well, she loves Spanish, but couldn't move away from sitting by Jules, so Samantha just tolerates her. Jules never apologized. She just moved on, and so did Samantha. Well, let's be clear. Samantha dropped her as a friend like a bad habit. Jules chose to hang with Melody, thinking it would help her climb the social ladder when, in reality, Jules is being used and abused by Melody. It's so weird because Samantha thought they were way better friends than that. Who knew her chronic disease would break them apart?

Rocco didn't appreciate how Jules stabbed his sister in her back by listening to Melody and hearing that Samantha was making life too difficult for Jules by saving a spot for her everyday—boo hoo—so Rocco broke off any communication with her. Samantha was frankly shocked but loved her brother for loving and supporting her.

And Bo? Well, he turned out to be a stellar human. He was so chill about their family rule. In fact, Bo thinks it's actually a good idea. I mean, who even does that these days… has dating rules?

He came over that Saturday night and played games with them all. And they've been hanging out ever since. Bo and Rocco hang together a lot, too, which is excellent, and Claire, Bo's sister, hangs out with Janey a lot, so Bo is always around.

The best news yet is that Samantha qualified to get a CGM—a continuous glucose monitor—just before Halloween. She's been so excited! Her diabetes management has been pretty up and down the past two months, which is very typical of T1D. In fact, it's called the teeter-totter disease because it does just that—it goes up and down.

Oh! At the end of September, Samantha got a really yucky virus and was sick for about five days. But believe it or not, that's what her pancreas needed cause it kicked her right out of the blasted honeymoon phase! Now, she can control her diabetes much more consistently… well, try to, at least, with insulin shots and blood checks and not having extra and random spurts of insulin trying to jack her up!

Bo's Uncle Justin is coming into town this weekend, and Samantha is invited to dinner to meet him and discuss diabetes. She hopes it's a good visit. She feels a bit nervous because she's so new to all of this and doesn't know what to ask him. Rocco has been helping her formulate some questions. Bo keeps telling her to be chill because Justin is very laid-back and the best uncle ever, so Samantha will try her best.

How's Melody? She's ridiculous, and who knows what lies she's been telling Jules? Thankfully, Samantha would only see her during lunch, and since she's been in with Nurse Howard, she hasn't had to see Melody at all.

Let's hope this good fortune continues because I have no intention of ever sitting by or talking to Melody ever again.

Okay, yeah, eating and hiding out isn't the bravest thing, but it has made life easier for Samantha not to have to let anyone know about her diabetes. Fortunately for her, Jules only told Melody, and Melody —after breaking Samantha's heart with her cruelty—moved on to torture and talk about anyone else she could talk about.

Samantha fully intends to rejoin the lunch crew when she has a pump. It's just too hard having to give herself shots then try and get to the cafeteria in a timely manner and get a place to sit.

Halloween is this Saturday. Samantha has her three-month check-up/CGM training on Friday after school. It just dawned on Samantha that trick-or-treating might not be such a great idea. It's hard to calculate all of those simple sugars! So, the Hansen family is gathering for their favorite time—dinner—and is planning Halloween this Thursday night since it will look very different for Samantha.

"So, CGM this Friday, eh, Samantha?" Dad smiles at her from across the dinner table.

"I am so excited. One less thing to do for diabetes!"

The entire family voiced a loud cheer altogether. YAYYY!

"What does that mean, Samantha? That GC thingy?" Janey is so sweet and precious.

"Good question," Samantha says. "What this will do for me is allow me NOT to have to do a blood check physically. Instead, I will have to do that maybe once a week or so to make sure it's accurate. It's a little needle that goes under my skin and will look like a medical patch on my arm. I change it every three days. It's wireless and will connect to an app on my phone. It will automatically check my blood sugar constantly!! BLESS UP!!

"Hallelujah! What a great invention!!" her mom says with great sincerity.

"K, so Halloween. Janey needs to go out trick-or-treating, and if Rocco still wants to go as old as he is, then go for it! As for me, I don't really care to go, nor do I want to. I'm thinking I can chill here and give the candy out. Maybe? Then, we can meet up after the trick-or-treating and watch a Halloween movie?" Samantha asks. She really doesn't care about candy that much. She never has, anyway, so it's not a big deal to her.

Rocco speaks up. "Okay, so Mom and Dad can take Janey, and I'm fine staying with Samantha to pass out candy, too."

"You're sure, Rocco?"

"Yeah, for sure. Should I have Bo come and hang with us, too? Unless he's hangin' with his sister and parents."

Their parents nod yes in unison.

"Okay, that's a great plan," their mom says. "Oh, and for Friday, Rocco, I'll need to pick Samantha up as soon as school lets out. Then, we will head to Dallas Children's Hospital for her appointment and CGM training. Can you please get Janey on Friday, Rocco?"

"Of course. Just send me a reminder text, please!"

Everyone laughs, and they finish dinner and tag-team clean the kitchen. Samantha pauses and watches everyone move around and work together.

What would I do without these fantastic people? Not survive, that's what. I cannot imagine living my life with diabetes without all of them.

Samantha smiles and rejoins everyone.

Friday can't get here soon enough!!

19

SAMANTHA HAS BEEN SO busy with her diabetes, homework, and balancing the Jules-Melody situation with Bo that she hasn't thrifted for months. Retail therapy used to be her go-to stress reliever. Now? She's just trying to make it through each day without screwing her body up too much. Or her love life... which, thankfully, is still blooming like a spring flower. But on Saturday afternoon, Janey, her mom, and she will be thrifting and shopping at Target.

The past two months have made Samantha feel like she's been doing a doggy paddle around and around in a circle and can't get out of the pool! Managing her diabetes has been rough—so many ups and downs. The worst part has been the low blood sugars during classes.

Just last week, she felt awful during Spanish, of all the classes, so Jules could see how it goes for Samantha. In fact, Samantha was feeling so poorly that Signora Alba had Jules WALK Samantha down to Nurse Howard. They didn't even talk, just walked in silence. Samantha can fake it just fine when she and Jules are in class, but she hasn't been one-on-one with Jules in a couple of months. So, to say this was awkward would be an understatement.

Samantha and Jules got to Nurse Howard's office, and Jules opened the door for them, and they went in. Then she just stood there watching as Samantha checked her blood glucose level and grabbed two juice pouches from her drawer.

"Do you feel sick? When you're having a low blood sugar?"

Samantha didn't know Jules was still there. She looks up in shock. "Yeah. I feel really crappy. My stomach hurts, and I feel super woozy like I could pass out."

"Oh. That sucks."

"Pretty much. You don't have to wait for me. I'm good. Thanks."

Jules slowly closes the office door.

"A friend of yours?" Nurse Howard asks sarcastically.

"Was, but no longer. Jules chose to share my personal information with a not-very-nice person who immediately tried to make me feel awful and lame for having a chronic disease. I shut her down and have been having lunch in here daily."

"Ahh," the nurse says. "Makes so much more sense now."

"Yep. Hey, I'm feeling good now. I'm ready to go back."

"Sure thing. And hey, Samantha? If you need to talk, you know I'm here."

"Thank you. I appreciate it."

Samantha smiles and grabs the BEEN IN THE NURSE'S OFFICE preprinted slip off the copies pile.

She was thinking about Jules's question. She'd never even asked how Samantha had felt before today. And maybe that's because Samantha has kept it all to herself. But like her plan has been the whole time, she intends to keep it to herself until she can get her CGM and a pump. Then, she feels like she can handle sharing about her disease. Perhaps Samantha's choosing not to tell Jules when she was first diagnosed put up a block or barrier in their friendship without her knowing.

It was a very sensitive time. I was overwhelmed and could barely even talk about it with my parents, Rocco, and Janey, let alone Jules, and obviously not Bo either. Nonetheless, you'd think your best friend would have your back. And be understanding. I don't know how she's changed so much since we started school this year. It's only been three months, or less than three months. And I will not take the blame for her sharing my secret with

Melody. I'm sure Melody coaxed it out of her because that's how Melody acts, but you'd think having been friends for four years would make for a much better base than some flighty, talkative, popular girl in high school.

* * *

"It's Fri-yayyyyy!" Samantha exclaims as she walks into the kitchen, ready to get her breakfast and get on the way to school. "Today's the day!" Samantha said happily, grabbing her oatmeal packet, bowl, and banana. She hasn't varied her breakfast very much, except it may be adding a different fruit for a different oatmeal flavor. Samantha is making herself stick to the same amount of carbs in the morning so that she can live her best life at school until lunchtime.

Her mom smiles at her. "I am super proud of you, sweetie. I know this has been anything but easy. But I'm sure glad we have such great technology these days that your doctor and clinic can get all your blood sugar numbers and insulin doses from the computer. And this is why you get your CGM. Because overall, you've kept your diabetes under the best control as you could."

"Aww thanks, Mom. You know I couldn't do this without you, Dad, Rocco, and Janey. I am so grateful for y'all."

Rocco pops into the kitchen. Followed by Dad and Janey.

"Good morning family!" Rocco announces as he enters.

Everyone gives a unified "morning," as they all continue to bustle around getting lunches ready, eating and finishing their breakfast, and rinsing dishes.

"Let's go, Samantha!"

"I'm ready, dude. Duh." But Samantha laughs as she follows him to the Honda.

Nothing will get me down today, no matter what. I won't let anything bug me. Also, why I didn't have this one thought dominating all of my thoughts is a mystery to me—oh wait, diabetes happened—but I WILL BE SIXTEEN on December 18!! Which means I CAN GO OUT ALONE WITH BO! Despite having so much going on with my blasted diabetes and high school homework, my thoughts of Bo thread through all of my day. And he's been around a lot. My parents really like him, and obvi he and Rocco are tight. And many times, he brings his little sis, Claire, to come and hang with Janey, too. I mean, what more could a girl ask for? I feel like I have little heart bubbles surrounding me at all times. Oh! And art class is AMAZE! We don't always get to be partners together, but I can at least gaze at his beautiful face in class. It's the cherry on top of all that's been happening and many times difficult—depending on my lovely diabetes—days!

And before she knows it, Samantha is in sixth-period Spanish and had to see Jules. Ever since she watched her blood check, drink her juices, and ask her questions last month, she seems to be making an effort with Samantha. But no way is Samantha going to cave that quickly. Jules broke her trust… broke their long-time friendship. Broke her possible love interest with her brother. Samantha can only think of the line from one of the songs from Wicked: I hope you're happy now, Jules!

Sure. That sounds a little harsh, but as Samantha has been negotiating high school with every other student, she's also been fighting a daily battle to maintain her diabetes, which is anything but easy! And as much as Bo and Samantha get to hang out, talk, play games, or talk together, there's nothing like having a bestie to share everything with!

"Hey Samantha, how's your day been?"

Samantha looks surprised as she turns toward Jules. "Good," Samantha answers shortly and to the point.

"So, are you doing anything fun for Halloween? I'm good with Melody, Hannah, and a few other peeps trick or treating."

"Awesome. Having a family meal of chili and cornbread, then Rocco, Bo, and I will give the candy out to the trick-or-treaters. Candy isn't really my friend now that I have diabetes."

Samantha says this last part with apparent smugness as if to say: *Jules, if you were my friend still and gave a crap, then you'd know this.*

But Jules just keeps on babbling. "Oh, that will be fun for you, Bo, and Rocco. Speaking of Rocco, how's he doing?" Jules ends this question shyly, knowing darn well that she blew it with Rocco and Samantha.

"Awesome. Rocco and Bo hang out all the time. They have some classes together and are trying out again for the high school soccer team. He seems really happy!"

"Oh! That's nice."

Samantha is spared from having to say anything in response because Signora Alba split them into groups to discuss the novel they'd been studying. Thankfully, the story has English on one side and Spanish on the other, making reading comprehension even possible. Signora Alba chose *The Alchemist*. It's actually been a fabulous novel to read and study.

The novel discussion takes up the bulk of class time. Samantha has truly enjoyed this class, and her most favorite period is next—Art with Bo!

Samantha was packing her stuff to head to Art and subconsciously waves happily to Jules as she sees her exiting the class. Jules waves back with a genuine smile.

CRAP! I'm supposed to do everything I can to NOT engage with Jules. However, this situation makes my heart sad because my mind and heart have always loved Jules, and now I'm dealing with all of this—stupid Melody. Plus, I know Melody will soon pull something really cruel, and Jules will come crawling back to me. I'm just waiting for that to happen. What will I do?

Samantha thinks these thoughts without focusing on where she's going. She almost runs into Melody, who's heading to whatever class she has for seventh period.

"Oh, if it isn't Disease Girl! Sorry to take Jules from you, oh, but I'm really not sorry cause Jules and Hannah do anything I want them to do. They're like my little puppets. It's amazing."

Samantha scrunches her face into a grumpy expression and is about to respond, but it is too late because Melody has entered her class.

If I were a cussing girl, I'd have a lot of cussy words to say right now! She, for real, makes me so angry! Argh!

Samantha takes three deep breaths as she enters the Art room. Bo is already in class. Samantha feels like she's on fire, and—her cheeks feel so hot! Hopefully, no one notices. Bo's back is turned away from

Samantha, so she sits and continues to breathe deeply, letting her anger blow out of her.

Remember I said that nothing would get me down today? Well, I forgot about the existence of Melody! But I'm feeling calmer. If I can breathe it out, then I'll be okay-ish. I actually feel bad for Jules. And Hannah. Who wants to be friends with someone like Melody? And yes, perhaps it was a bit dramatic to stop talking or interacting with Jules, but she betrayed me by telling Melody my personal info. Whatever. I need to paint!

Samantha is calm enough to complete today's class assignment, which is to paint an abstract painting with repetition of a basic, everyday item. Samantha chooses a piggy bank from Ms. Love's possible choices for the class. And much to Samantha's elation, Ms. Love said they could sit anywhere today! While gathering her supplies, she returned to her easel and placed it at one of the large art tables to see Bo set up right next to her. Yeah. This class will end her day perfectly.

Sigh.

Samantha gives Bo a sweet smile, and they commence their project and ease into casual conversation about this and that.

"Hey, isn't your doctor's appointment for what you'll get today? I'm sorry. I can't remember what it's called!"

"It is. It's fine. It's not a common abbreviation for people to just roll off of their tongues. It's called a CGM, or a continuous glucose monitor. My mom is picking me up right after class. Then, we'll head to Dallas Children's Hospital. I have my three-month check-up, and we will stay overnight with training later today and more in the morning. Then, I'm in business! I'm so excited. This CGM will really help me take care of diabetes way better."

"Incredible." Bo gives Samantha a sincerely content smile.

Soul melt. Be still my heart. Butterfly flutters. Sighhh. The way this boy makes me feel....

Samantha can only smile and turn toward her canvas to continue sketching in pencil. Ms. Love's rules are that pencil is always first, followed by sharpies, paint, markers, and so forth, so she's almost finished her sketching part.

Samantha takes a peek at Bo's canvas. He chose a ruler as his object.

Interesting! I like how he's positioned the rulers. It is very arty.

"Bo! You're really artistic. Have you taken classes or drawn before this class?"

"Thanks, Samantha. All I've learned has been from my mom. She's a fabulous watercolorist, and I asked her to teach me art last year, and we've been working on it together. Having taken lessons previously is the sole reason I took this class—because I've been taught by a professional—otherwise, no way! I was awful before my mom taught me. But what about you? You're also very artistic."

"Aw, thanks. I am self-taught. I started doodling and drawing about five years ago. I found it really therapeutic and calming for me. Sometimes, I will draw and draw and draw. I did this a lot when I got diagnosed. Helped me sort through things emotionally a lot better."

"That's great. I am so glad you've got something to help you. I know it's been pretty hard and awful for you these past three months. And I'm sorry, Samantha."

Bo is staring right into Samantha's eyes, at this point, and she can feel electricity coming from her head to her toes and back again. She's trying to hold back tears because it's been so complicated and sucky!

20

"It's been a lot, I'll just say that much," Samantha says and turns back to her canvas.

Bo gently reaches his arm out and gives her a gentle hug. She leans her head into him. More electricity flowing through her body! They've not been very physically touchy with each other to this point, so this was a step in the right direction, for sure. Bo retracts his arm, and Samantha, now composed, turns back to look at Bo's gorgeous face. She could stare at him all day!

"Thanks for being so supportive, Bo. To be honest, I was afraid you'd have no interest in me anymore since, you know, I'm diseased—as Melody called me."

"Pfff, not a chance. I'm not that shallow." He guffaws and continues, "Who the heck is Melody?"

"Oh, just one of the popular sophomores. Melody attended middle school with Jules and me, and now, why, I don't even know nor understand, she has her vice grip on Jules. Anyway, enough of all that. I appreciate you very much." Samantha gives him her best smile, and they both turn to continue their project.

Bo is easy to talk with, so they talk about colors, shapes, and positioning for their project for the rest of the period. The time whizzes by, which is both a pro and a con! Samantha could feel herself liking this boy more and more.

Do I want to do this? Fall for this, Bo? Am I being silly since I'm still 15?

But she knows the answer.

Heck yes!

Bo is all she can think about these days. He permeates her every thought, not like freaky or anything, just he's sweetly in her thoughts constantly, which she thoroughly enjoys!

BZZZZZ

Samantha feels her phone vibrate. It's her mom!

Mom: *"I'm here. In front of the school"*

"Gotta go! Thanks again for being so supportive, Bo. For real, it means a lot to me."

"My pleasure. Um, so do you want to text me later when you've finished your training? I didn't want to text you cause I didn't want to distract you ladies or anything, ya know?"

"I sure will! Bye, Bo!" Samantha dashes out of the classroom and heads toward the front of the school.

Samantha is walking even more rapidly now, searching for their SUV.

Bingo!

When Samantha's mom sees her, she moves to the curb. Samantha opens the middle car door and flings her backpack in. Then, she opens the passenger side door and jumps in. "Let's go!"

"And hello to you too, precious!"

They laugh together, feeling true joy for this afternoon appointment and the training and overnight stay.

"How was your day?"

"Let's just say that I survived the evil Melody today, and Jules being Jules, but finished the day painting with Bo, so it ended fabulously. Oh! I had two high blood sugars today, which really sucked cause I couldn't eat lunch until just the end of the lunch period. Then, I was high again just before you got me. I corrected."

"I brought a little cooler just in case of lows and highs, so I have some zero-sugar sodas in there, too, with some more juice pouches."

"Oh, thanks Mom. I need a zero-sugar drink for sure and more water! I feel so dehydrated, and my head is spinning a bit!!"

"My poor girl! I'm so sorry. You know, Samantha, if I could do anything to take this away from you, I would."

"I know, Mom. I know."

Samantha opens and starts to drink her zero-sugar drink as she and her mom fall into a comfortable silence. It will take them about forty-five minutes to get to the hospital from her high school.

When Samantha can no longer bear her thoughts, she connects her phone and put on her faves list, songs that make her float away from all problems. All cumbersome thoughts. Anything that is bringing her down. This particular playlist has become her saving grace since her diagnosis. Anytime she's been feeling the least bit overwhelmed, she's been throwing on her headphones and soaking in every song. Every drumbeat, every instrument, the vocalists, the lyrics--all of it!!

Samantha rests her head on her seat and closes her eyes. Her mom reaches over and rubs her arm. Samantha knows her mom or her dad would gladly take this disease in for her if at all possible. But as Samantha knows well enough, especially since she is fifteen years old, that this disease was hers to own, maintain, and control as best as she can. Dr. Swaneyard's words, more often than not, pass through her mind when she least expects it. "Don't fight your diabetes because it will win. Instead, know where your blood glucose levels are at and maintain and control them to the best of your ability."

"Samantha! Wake up, sweetie. We're here."

Samantha feels a gentle shaking in her arm. "That was so fast!"

"That's because you were out! Ready to go in?"

"Yep. Let me grab my small bag in my backpack."

Samantha unzips her backpack and wiggles her arm around until she finds her small fanny pack containing her glucose monitor, a snack, and a juice pouch. She gets out of the passenger seat and joins her mom as they walk toward the physician's office part of the hospital.

Today's checkup will include a huge test called the A1CG. This test will give an average of her blood glucose numbers for the past three months. She will discuss any trends that they see. If there are a lot of lows at a particular time, highs at a specific time, or a good average number, then she has her insulin doses dialed in okay. But if not, they look at all these trends, including the doctor and the nurses, and will adjust what will work best for Samantha. The whole goal is to mimic the pancreas. As mentioned, Samantha's pancreas no longer emits insulin to break down the food she eats into glucose to go into her cells to give her energy to feed her body. And so the shots, for now, mimic her pancreas. Once she gets the pump, the CGM and the insulin pump will be even better. Besides having insulin cell transplants, that is about as close as you can get to mimic the human pancreas.

Samantha does not feel nervous about going to this appointment today because she does know she has tried her very best. The honeymoon screws up everything. So, she's very happy to be out of that, even though being sick for five days was less than ideal. She also knows that all she can do is give her best. This disease will always be up and down, but getting the CGM today will be a step in the very right direction. Coupled with getting the insulin pump in a few more months, it will be the closest thing to mimicking a human pancreas, which is amazing.

She was thinking to herself the other day that she was sure glad that Samantha was older when she got diagnosed other than being younger, because at least she understands what's happening with her body or what has happened. Now, one thing that she is going to deal with that younger kids don't deal with when they get diagnosed is the wonderful world of hormones. They especially tend to skew blood sugar, and as she gets older, and she is to get married, and when she has kids, her pregnancy and getting pregnant will also affect her diabetes and blood glucose levels.

But one thing at a time.

"Samantha Hansen."

Samantha and her mom get up and go to the nurse, who will take them back to take her weight and blood pressure vitals, and then they will wait to see Dr. Swaneyard.

"Hello, Samantha. Let's have you step on the scale so we can get your weight, please. And your height while you're there."

Samantha steps on the scale, and the nurse records the number. Then, she gets measured.

"Okay, your weight looks great. You've gained at least five pounds back, which is excellent. You've grown a half inch since you lost about ten pounds."

"Okay, awesome. That means I'm five foot eight and a half inches."

Samantha or her mom talk about Samantha's height while the nurse checks her vitals. Then, the nurse takes them both to room number five to wait for Dr. Swaneyard.

"Okay, Samantha," the nurse says. "Are there any changes you want to talk to me about, like how you're feeling or any issues with food, shots, or anything else?"

"Well, I survived the first few months of my sophomore year, so I can consider that a win. The only thing that has been a little difficult has been having a low or high blood sugar at school and having to go to the office for a blood check and to pump up or to correct with insulin. Also, I'm eating lunch in the nurse's room because it's taking me a while to get back into the cafeteria after I've done a blood check and my shot. So, having the CGM will be amazing for me. I am looking forward to it today so much. I can hardly wait."

"Oh, I'm sorry to hear all that," the nurse says. "I know a lot of the kids always tell us that it takes time, especially when you're still on shots. But this too shall pass. Because now you're getting this CGM today. And hopefully, in another three to six months, you qualify for an insulin pump. And then you can eat with everybody else. And that would be the best thing for you ever. I know this takes extra work right now, and we appreciate your diligence. Because I know you didn't ask for diabetes, nor did anybody else diagnosed with T1D, but we commend you for your hard work."

Samantha looks at her mom and they smile. Samantha and her mom know that they had worked hard. It has not been easy, but this diabetes, the shots, and the blood checks have been a lot, especially in her second year of high school.

"Okay, ladies. Everything looks good, so I will let Dr. Swinney know that you're here, and he will be around just a bit. When you finish your appointment, Samantha, I believe Nurse Beth will be on shift for your CGM training. We let her know that you were coming in, and we know that she was there when you got first diagnosed. So, hopefully, that will make this whole new situation even better."

"Oh, my gosh, you're the best, and you've made me so happy. That was very nice of Nurse Beth and very nice of you guys. I know that's not easy for her since she only works a few shifts per week because she has three kids, so that was pretty cool. Thank you."

Samantha already thinks she will draw a thank you card for Nurse Beth and her family because that would be pretty cool. She's not sure how many nurses do that type of thing for their patients, but she surely appreciates it.

Samantha's mom sits back in her chair and pulls out her book, and Samantha pulls out her phone to text Bo. You never know how long it will take to wait for Dr. Swaneyard because he is very busy. These appointments get stacked back-to-back with all the kids who come in every three months.

Samantha: *"Hey, at the doctor's office. I grew half an inch and gained five pounds. That's something that usually a teen girl would never be excited about. But I am since I lost about ten pounds. Waiting for Dr. Swaneyard to come in, and after this checkup, I'll go upstairs to the third floor again, and then I'll text you after we get trained on the CGM. Hope you're having a nice afternoon."*

Bo: *"Ha. You're right. No teen girl would ever say they're excited to gain five pounds. Cool, you grew a half inch. Okay, thanks for texting. Talk to you later."*

21

Samantha puts her phone away because Dr. Swaneyard doesn't like to have phones out when they're talking.

There's a light knock on their door.

"Come in," Samantha says.

"Well, hello, Hansen ladies! OK, Your A1CG overall average is 8.5. Now, don't panic. We want to aim for below six, but remember, you are a newly diagnosed T1D, and you just came out of your honeymoon. So those are all factors to take into consideration. But well done. Because it could be higher and it's not. So, I'm looking over all of your records and numbers, and it looks like, for the most part, you've kept up with your regular blood glucose checks and shots. I see that lunchtime has been less than ideal, and I'm sorry about that. And coming to the office to see the nurse is always a pain in the neck, but it will get better, and today is the first step to getting better and less invasive in your life."

Samantha and her mom smile because they are definitely happy about this today. This is a big step, and her whole family is excited for her to have this CGM.

One day, Jules and I will be friends again, and then I can share these things with her. I hope that happens, even if I'm still grumps about what she did to me.

"So, now that you're going to get the CGM today. Would you think you'll never do a physical blood glucose check again?"

Everybody laughed because, no, that is not the case. It's important to keep calibrated with the blood glucose monitor.

"I'll take it from our laughter that you know that's not the case. And that's why it is an important part that requires maturity on your part. Number one, the CGM will make a huge difference in your life. Number two, it is a machine, and it still can have flaws. So, this means you will want to keep up with all of your shots, and now your blood glucose machine will record all the blood checks it does, which is pretty cool. You will still have low and high blood sugars, and sometimes you may not feel well, but your blood sugar numbers look good. So that's the time when I would do a blood check. Or you may have a high blood sugar and feel okay or not know that you're okay—same thing—check it."

He smiles and continues. "So, like I said, this CGM will make a huge difference and will make you feel much freer, take less time, and be less invasive. But it also means you must keep monitoring your machine and such. Now, enough about that. It looks like you gained weight, and your half inch—that's awesome. You should be able to gain another five pounds in the next five months, so that will get you back to your weight, which was good for your height and age. I'm not going to fret about weight too much because your hormones will continue to kick in more and affect you more and affect your blood sugar more. As you continue the next few months, you may see that your blood sugar will be all over the place. Hormones affecting blood sugar levels are very typical in a teen girl because hormones will skew the blood sugar. I don't want you to worry about it. You may run a bit higher for a year, so we will work with it as best as possible."

"Well, that sounds less than ideal," Samantha says. "So, do I just do the best I can? Do I need to do something different to improve it or help myself?"

"Nope, other than doing your very best to keep your blood sugars between 70 and 150. That's your only job. And like I said, if you find that you're running a bit higher for a few months, and that's okay. Just let it go because hormones are really tricky to work with when you're giving yourself insulin compared to the pancreas' still spread out insulin."

"Okay," Samantha says. "I appreciate you telling me about that because I probably would've freaked out thinking that something's going on or I'm not doing my best if my blood sugars are all over the place."

"Another thing I don't know if we discussed very much is exercise and diabetes—they are difficult friends together, but also good friends together. This means that exercise is good for you and can and will help your body use less insulin, which is a good thing. However, it can also be difficult not to get low blood sugar or something like that. If you have high blood sugar, it's not good to exercise, but only a few cases will make it difficult. Are you taking PE at school?"

"I was going to, but once I got diagnosed, I switched and am taking an art class, which I love. I just have to take something my junior and senior year for PE."

"Okay, that was probably a good idea since you were newly diagnosed this summer. We will work through exercise as you go along. If you could, I would like you to go walking. That would be great since you're healthy and active."

"Okay, that will not be a problem," she says. "We actually have a really nice pond in our neighborhood. Maybe you and I can walk every day together, Mom?"

"I think I would love that. Luckily, living in Texas, for the most part, the weather is very good every single day. Except for when it's scorching hot or a little cold, but you know what I mean."

The doctor nods. "Okay, that's everything I need to discuss with you today. So onward and upward, and I'm super excited for you to get the CGM. I am on shift to come in and see patients tomorrow morning, so I will be over and see you before you check out. Would that be okay? "

"We would just love to see you, Dr. Swaneyard. We appreciate you taking such good care of Samantha," her mom says pleasantly.

"Yeah, for sure, Dr. Swaneyard. Whatever works for your schedule is fine with me. I appreciate you taking good care of me and helping me learn to care for myself."

"All right, that sounds good, ladies. I will have Nurse Andrea come and get you and take you both upstairs."

"Okay, thank you. I will see you tomorrow," her mom says, turning to Samantha. "Once we get settled in our room, I'll go to the car and get the duffel bag you packed last night—and my bag, too. Does that sound okay?

"Sounds good to me." Samantha smiles when she says this.

Nurse Andrea taps lightly on the door, and Samantha tells her to come in. She and her mom gather their items, go out the door, and follow Andrea out of the room and the office to the elevators.

"Okay, ladies, I'll take it to your room once we get to the third floor. And then Miss Beth will talk to you about your procedure to learn how to do the CGM."

"Thanks, Andrea," Samantha's mom says.

Samantha nods. "Yeah, thanks so much, Andrea."

The elevator beeps, and all three women exit onto the third floor. Suddenly, Samantha is feeling a little bit nervous. She will have to put the CGM into her arms or stomach or the upper part of her butt for three days. She's hoping it won't be too painful to wear or hurt very much to insert. She also hopes to acclimate to this new invasion of her body sooner rather than later.

Andrea takes them to the nurses' station, where they all greet Nurse Beth, who then takes them down the hall. While walking to room 314, Samantha passes the room she was in when she first got diagnosed three months ago.

At least this time, I'm not a newly diagnosed type one diabetic, and I am getting something very wonderful that will help me.

"Okay, here's your room, ladies. I will be back."

"Okay, thanks, Nurse Beth. I'm going to run to the car and get our duffel bags," Samantha's mom says. She waves to Samantha and walks out with Nurse Beth.

* * *

HALLOWEEN

"Hey guys! We're home!" Samantha yells as she enters the door from the garage.

"Hey, sis, welcome back!" Rocco walks through the kitchen, comes over to Samantha, and hugs her. "How did it all go?"

"Training was great but exhausting! Mom and I had to practice putting in the CGM needle. Ugh. It was hard work, but we got it, and I did it alone today! See?" She lifts her sleeve to reveal the oval-shaped device. "I need to change it every three or four days, but wow! It is so awesome. Let me show you what it tells me via the app."

Samantha pulls out her phone, and Dad and Janey join Rocco and Samantha as she shows them how her blood glucose levels appear. The blood sugar numbers are sent digitally from the GCM.

* * *

SAMANTHA'S MOM WATCHES HER FAMILY WITH A SWEET SMILE ON HER face. No, it's not a cure, but boy, is it a step in the right direction. Her mom gazes with pride at Samantha. These past three months have been rough! Annie is amazed at her daughter's bravery and forza. Who wants a chronic disease? Absolutely no one—yet, this sweet fifteen-year-old has embraced this new and difficult lifestyle change so much better than she could imagine! Annie loves to see Samantha smiling more than fretting, happy more than depressed. Now, it doesn't mean that won't come, and it has come off and on and in waves, but Annie is glad to see more smiles than tears.

* * *

Samantha, Janey, and their mom take off for their thrifting date together before making chili and cornbread, getting the candy ready to hand out, and, best of all, dressing up!

"Oh my gosh! This dress is sooo cute, Mom. What do you think?" Samantha holds up an adorable floral tiered dress.

"Oh, it is so cute! You always find the best clothing items! Janey, did you find anything yet?"

"Yeah, Mom, I found a few T-shirts and the cutest skirts."

The three of them continue oohing and ahhing over so many items until they whittle down their pile of treasures to a reasonable amount.

"Okay, ladies, let's check out and get home! We have a lot to do to prepare for Halloween night!"

"Okay, I'm ready!" Samantha puts her items on the counter, and Janey does, too.

"Janey! Those skirts are darling! You're going to look great in them!"

"Thanks, Sammie!" Janey gave her the biggest smile.

She's really growing up more and more. It's been way more fun to have these types of outings together with her and Mom since Janey turned ten in August.

And now, home to get ready to see Bo! That's literally all I can think of. Texting back and forth last night was so amazing for a while. Bo is so wonderful and hot! I know that sounds so cheesy, but he is! He is nice and funny, and I think he cares about me. I'm feeling that more and more each day. And I like him more and more and more each day. I'm glad Bo will hang with us tonight. He will bring Claire, his little sister, and she will trick or treat Mom, Dad, and Janey. And Bo, Rocco, and I can just hang together for a good few hours.

Do I wish we could be alone? Yeah. Not gonna lie. Those thoughts are getting more and more frequent in my mind. I want it to be December 18th. Could it just get here already?! Dang. Waiting until I'm sixteen is taking forever!

22

SAMANTHA, Janey, and her mom make it home and join her dad and Rocco in preparing dinner, filling the candy bowl, and getting dressed! Two hours later, everyone had eaten and put on their Halloween garb just as Bo and Janey ring the doorbell camera.

"Come on guys! Bo and Claire are here! It's candy time!"

"Wahoo!!" Janey yells as she hugs Claire. The girls dressed up as babies, in footie pajamas, ponytails, bows, and huge pacifiers around their necks.

"Oh my gosh! You two are precious. Please let me take a photo of you!" Samantha takes a few pictures of the girls.

"Okay! Let's go girls. Have fun you three!"

Their parents wave goodbye to the three of them and go out the front door as Rocco, Bo, and Samantha set up camp chairs in the driveway. It's one of Samantha's fave Texas traditions: good weather on Halloween calls for driveway talking and passing out candy! Rocco and Bo have dressed up as Pokémon characters, and Samantha is dressed as Trelawney from Harry Potter.

"Okay, boys, here come the kiddos!" Samantha says as she points down her street. Their house, nestled in a cul-de-sac, makes for good neighbor camaraderie. The three of them wave to their neighbors on both sides.

"So Samantha, how was thrifting today?"

"Thank you for asking, Bo. I found a few adorable items!" Samantha gleamed.

Rocco rolls his eyes and laughs. "Bo, do not encourage her! She *always* finds something to buy everywhere she goes!" Rocco laughs while saying this because he loves to tease Samantha as much as he can. He's chilled out since Samantha's diagnosis, but today, he can see a noticeable difference in her face. She has a look of relief, and her features look softer, so in that case, he's ready to amp up the teasing again!

"Oh please, just cause I'm not buying video games or new controllers doesn't mean you're not buying stuff, weirdo!"

"Okay, okay, you two, knock it off!" Bo chides them. "Plus, more kids are coming!"

The banter continues between the three of them, and they give out all the candy the entire time. Samantha takes note of the various times that Bo has softly touched her hand or arm, which, for real, gives her a zillion tingles!

I'm pretty sure he likes me. Should I ask Rocco? I don't want to come across as some desperate girl, though. Maybe I should just keep on keepin' on until my b-day, and aww, what happens when I turn sixteen?

Samantha can't help but think of these things. It's hard out there for a girl when she likes someone and wants to be sure that boy likes her BACK! Samantha tries not to overthink it all. But she's not so good at that.

She sees her parents coming back, along with Janey and Claire. "Hey, cutie girls! How was it?"

"We got so much candy!" both girls yell excitedly.

"Score!" Bo chimes in. "Got any to share with your adorable older brother?" He gives Claire a cute little wink and a smile.

Claire digs in her bag and gives Bo a handful.

"Aw, thanks, little sister! You're so nice to me!" Then he turns toward everyone.

"Thanks, Hansen family. We both had such a fun night! I'm gonna take this girl home to get to bed. Umm, Rocco and Samantha, you guys up for hanging out tomorrow, maybe playing some video games?"

"Yeah!" Rocco answers happily.

"Sure thing! And thanks for hanging with us tonight." Samantha kind of gushes out that last part of her sentence. She blushes and quickly turns her head toward Janey. "Let's see what candy you got, Miss Janey," Samantha tries to say casually as she, Rocco, and Janey wave goodbye to Bo and Claire.

They head inside, where Janey dumps everything onto the floor and starts sorting it into the same type of candies. She bags them up and goes to bed. Their mom and dad go upstairs to bed, too.

Rocco is still downstairs, so he gestures to Samantha to come into the kitchen with him. "Ice cream sis?"

"Yeah, I'd love some!"

"Oh, yummo. Chocolate toffee!" he says into the open freezer.

"Yes! My fave!"

They both sit to eat, and Samantha measures out her amount so she knows the carbs.

"So, you know Bo really digs you, right?" her brother asks.

"He does?" Samantha feigns surprise, but she's definitely blushing.

"But you know this already, don't ya?"

"I mean, I was hoping he did!"

"Well, let's say we discuss it. A lot." He laughs and gives Samantha a wry smile.

"You discuss me? I didn't think you dudes did stuff like that."

"Yeah, we sure do. We discuss you in texts or in between games, ha, ha."

"That's funny. I have to admit I hate not having Jules around. We talked about everything together. It was always so great!"

"Yeah," he agrees. "It sucks it ended up like this. I see Jules around school quite a bit. I say hi to her and boy! Does she look sad!"

"She made her choice."

"Yeah, I know. But I don't think it's going how Jules thought it would go, ya know?"

"How could it? Melody is the worst!"

"It's just dumb," he adds. "Jules chose Melody. I really liked her, ya know?"

"I know you did, Rocco and I'm sorry for you. It's stupid—all of it. I've had to push that whole situation away from me cause I can't give time to even fretting or thinking about it! It's too emotional for me." Samantha can feel she's on the verge of crying.

"Well, enough of that. But anyway. Bo totally digs you. That much I know."

"Thanks for telling me. I dig him, too, and I was hoping he liked me and that I was reading him right. He's a great guy," Samantha dreamily answers.

"Okay, okay. It's getting mushy. Let's go to bed already!"

They rinse their bowls, put them into the sink, and walk upstairs together.

"Sweet dreams, Rocco!"

"You, too. But don't even tell me if your dreams are about Bo. I don't want to hurl!"

Samantha punches his arm as he goes into his room. As she enters her room, she feel so relieved that Bo indeed likes her.

I mean, I'd hoped he liked me. But I didn't want to assume anything. I'm lucky that Bo and Rocco are good friends. It works fabulously for me!!

Samantha doses her ice cream snack, goes through her bedtime routine, and pulls out her sketchbook. She sketches a few flowers, rainbows, and other cute items, smiling the entire time with utter happiness! She plugs in her phone, puts up her sketchbook, and lies down, ready to go into dreamland—hoping her dreams are all about Bo!

23

Thanksgiving Break

"Hey, someone, get the door!" Samantha yells.

She and her mom are working on a puzzle. Tomorrow will be Thanksgiving Day, so she, Rocco, and Janey have been off school since the end of the school day last Friday.

"Anyone? Fine. I'll get it!" Samantha stomps to the front door. She peeks through the peephole.

Jules!?

Samantha opens the door slowly. She sees Jules crying before she can say anything snide and sarcastic.

"Jules? What in the world is going on? And why are you here at MY house?"

"Samantha, I'm sorry. I just didn't know what to do or where to go, and I subconsciously came here. To you. Can I come in?"

"Um, we're playing games as a family, but, I mean, I guess so."

What in the world? What can I even do? This feels very awkward. Why would Jules even pick me? Ugh, Let's see how this goes then.

"Come in and stand here for a minute. Let me tell my family that we need to go and talk in my room."

"Okay." Jules sniffs loudly. "Thanks, Samantha," Jules says tearfully.

Samantha walks into the family room and explains quickly about Jules and the need for them to talk together in her room.

"Oh! I'm so glad she came to you!" her mom replies happily.

Samantha rolls her eyes. "Yes, thank you, Mom," Samantha admits sarcastically.

"Are you sure, Samantha, you want to do this with Jules right now, tonight?" Rocco inquires quizzically with his hands up in the air.

"Yeah, it's okay. I'm okay. I need to really find out what the heck is going on with Jules. I'll be back in here in a while, guys."

Samantha goes back into the front entry of her house and motions to Jules to follow her upstairs to her room. They walk in silence all the way up. I mean, it's not like they've hung out or talked for months.

"Come on in, Jules. Take a seat in my chair. Do you need some water? And how did you get here?"

"Yes, please. I do need some water, and Bo dropped me here. I have a long story and am ready to tell you if you allow me."

"Go back to Bo giving you a ride," Samantha grumbles. "I need that answered first."

"Okay, okay. I ended up texting Bo for help. I was at a dumb party with Melody, Hannah, and some other people, and things got really, really out of control. It was as if I suddenly got knocked in the head, and I could see clearly for the first time that I was an idiot! Why was I even there? Why was I with these people? I've been utterly miserable for months. You've no idea," Jules mumbles sadly. "And I'm sorry, Samantha. I have so much to say to you! I have so much to apologize for. I have so much to fix. I wanted to go home, but it was weird. Bo said to me that you'd want to talk with me first." Jules starts to cry again. "And I was just so upset I didn't actually confirm that but didn't say no to the idea."

Samantha let Jules cry. She isn't going just to forgive and forget that quickly. Nope. Backstabbing hurts, and she doesn't care how badly Jules cries. She screwed Samantha over.

"Go on." Samantha firmly says and folds her arms. She figures Jules can be honest with her and tell the truth as to why she just up and dissed her.

"You're going to think I'm a literal idiot, which I am. So, remember the second or third day of school, when Melody was so rude to you and called you blood disease girl?" Samantha nods and glares at Jules.

She continues. "Well, Melody tricked me into telling her why you're always so late to lunch period. I don't even know how she got it out of me. Then she told me I could totally get that same blood disease, and I was so scared and was an idiot and went along with her stupidity and rudeness until tonight. I was afraid to get diabetes, but I didn't even ask you. I just believed Melody, and that was it! I still don't even know why. I'm really sorry, Samantha. I know that explanation can't possibly fix these past months when I've been a total idiot, so all I can continue to say is that I'm sorry a million billion times over!" Jules resumes sobbing.

Samantha sits still on her bed, pondering what she's heard from Jules.

I'm not sure what I think about all of this that Jules told me. Do I believe her? Is she that gullible? I didn't know she was, but obviously she is. Hmm.

"Anything else you'd like to share with me? Like why you dropped me like a scorching hot pop tart after we've been friends for five years? FIVE YEARS, Jules." Samantha raises her voice a few octaves, then resumes in a calmer tone. "That's a lot of time as best friends just to flush away, ya know?" She grits her teeth, growling this sentence out.

"I know Samantha, I know! And, and… well, you're always confident in the way you dress, talk, walk, and associate with others, You've got oodles of confidence! So much more than me, more than I've ever had. You don't care what others think. You are smart, kind, fun, and you're beautiful!"

Samantha is stunned. So much for knowing the true Jules! She had absolutely no idea Jules felt this way. What?

"Jules, woah, woah. What are you talking about? You've got to be kidding me! You're adorable. Sweet. Kind. Smart. I mean, where did you get all of this crap in your head? Have I made you feel this way somehow?" Samantha asks.

"What? You? No, no, no. It's all me, Samantha. I'm not like you. I'm the oldest of five. It's hard for my parents to buy the things I want or need since we have a lot of kids in the family, but that's not your fault. I'm dramatic about it. You've always shared everything with me, and look what I did. I let envy and jealousy creep in and guide my actions. I listened to a total selfish idiot and went along with her lies because I was weak, sad, and selfish, too. I've not been there for you with your T1D. What kind of friend does that to her best friend?" Jules begins to cry again… wracking sobs now.

Samantha has heard enough. It's time for her to move in and hug Jules. She gets up from her bed and goes to her chair, grabbing Jules's hand and standing her up—they're still the same height—and Samantha happily pulls Jules in for a hug. "Okay, enough already. Let's get you calmed down, okay?"

"Okkaayy," Jules mutters through her tears.

Samantha holds onto Jules for a long while before backing out of the hug. "Come on, let's go get some ice cream! We've got a whole bunch of flavors. And Jules?"

"Yes, Samantha?"

"Of course I forgive you. Thanks for being honest with me, though. That is an important thing—total honesty and transparency. Now, let's let the tears go, and if you're up to it, let's rejoin my family, okay? Oh! Do your parents know where you are?"

"Yes, yes, I texted them that my plans had changed, and I was going to your house instead."

Well! I sure didn't expect all of that to come out of her mouth. Wow. I never, ever knew she felt this way about me about herself, and I see she was just being dumb hanging with Melody. Thank goodness that's over. I will happily text Bo when Jules goes home tonight to thank him. I think he knew Jules and I needed to fix our relationship and that we needed each other. Wow. Bo is something amazing.

Samantha and Jules walk down the stairs and into the kitchen. They pass Samantha's family—still playing games—and she sees their eyes curiously follow her and Jules as they walk into the kitchen. Samantha gives them all a thumbs-up, smiles, and continues to walk toward the kitchen and straight to the freezer.

"Grab a seat, Jules, and I'll dish us both up. Are you okay with chocolate almond ice cream from Broom's?"

"Yes, please." Jules sniffles her response, and Samantha grabs a water bottle and a box of Kleenex. She slides both items in front of Jules.

"Here, Jules. Drink up!" Samantha encouraged her.

Samantha grabs two bowls, two spoons, and the ice cream. As she's dishing a portion for each of them, she happens to turn her head toward her family. Her mom looks right at her, smiling like the Cheshire cat in Alice in Wonderland. Their kitchen and family room make one great room, so it's not hard to have everyone know what's happening with each other. Samantha smiles back, puts a spoon in each bowl, hands one to Jules, and sits her bowl down on the counter beside Jules.

"Glad to have you back in my life, Samantha. I'm sorry for any pain and hurting your heart that I caused you." Jules takes in a spoonful of ice cream after she delivers this statement.

"Yeah, not gonna lie. It hasn't been great for me, but what's done is done. But I do wish you had confided in me about everything you shared with me earlier. I never look at you as less than me. Never. If anything, I've also looked at us as equals in everything—our academic interests, how we dress, what we do in our spare time, and all," Samantha reassures her.

"Yeah, well, you're a better person than I am for that sole reason." Jules lets out a long sigh. "Why is it that chocolate almond ice cream can solve all things?" Jules laughs.

"For real! I love this ice cream!" Samantha agrees and smiles broadly at Jules.

They continue to chat, just like they used to. Jules finally stops sniffling, and all tears have finally dissipated. Eventually, Samantha's whole family migrates to the counter, and more ice cream scoops are placed in more bowls. Soon, everyone is laughing and chatting for a long while together.

Rocco doesn't initiate too much with Jules, though. He keeps himself at the other end of their large counter, probably still wary of what had all gone down between his sister and Jules, with all of it still very raw in his mind.

24

As the night winds down. Samantha asks if Rocco wouldn't mind taking Jules home. He kind of gives Samantha a "what the heck look?" but complies, nonetheless.

"Sure thing! Let's go, girls!" Rocco replies as upbeat as he can pretend to be feeling. He'll definitely be chatting with his sister after this little stunt.

"Oh, please don't go to any trouble, you guys. Let me text my parents to see who can come and get me."

"Nah, it's cool, Jules. We'll take you." Rocco gives Jules a half smile. The three of them start toward the front door, where Samantha and Rocco's mom comes to Jules and gives her a huge hug.

"Glad you came over tonight, Jules. You've been missed." She smiles and waves as the three of them go out to the Honda.

Samantha jumps into the front seat, not wanting to make it awkward between Rocco and Jules. "So, what are your family plans for the rest of the week, Jules?" Samantha inquires.

"Pretty chill. My cousins, aunt, and uncle should come from Utah later tonight. So, we'll all hang out, eat, go to the movies, etc. It's the one family where all their kids are the same age as us."

"Yeah, sure, I remember them. Well, that's fun. Maybe we can find a time or two to get together, all of us?" Samantha gestures at the three of them and mentions this idea.

"I'd love that you guys. I've missed you both—a lot," Jules comments with sincerity.

"We're here, girls," Rocco emphasizes as he pulls into Jules's driveway.

"Bye, y'all! Happy Thanksgiving! Samantha, are you okay with us starting to text each other again?" Jules asks quietly.

"Absolutely." Samantha gets out of the Honda and joins Jules so she can walk her to the front door. They give each other a huge hug and then part ways.

Samantha is still smiling as she gets into the car. "Thanks, Rocco. I'm sorry if any part of this situation was awkward for you. I realized that was possible on the drive to Jules's house. Oops!" Samantha grins sheepishly in the hopes that Rocco will be forgiving to her.

"Yeah, glad that finally dawned on you. It's cool. I didn't want to rekindle anything with Jules because this is all new with you two. I'm not gonna lie, though. I still like her. I never stopped, but I wasn't going to hang with someone who wasn't friends with you anymore," Rocco elaborates as they continue to drive back home.

"I figured you did that for me, and I thank you. I'm sorry if things are still messed up with you two, and I do hope you can sort it out, ya know?"

"It's okay. I will give it some time and be an outside observer to see how I feel about her apology and such."

"Agreed. I'm just so happy. So relieved. It's sucked without Jules by my side, especially with my dang T1D!" Samantha tells Rocco as they slowly walk into their house.

"Well, that was most unexpected, was it not?" Their mom retorts when she sees them.

"Uh, yeah, one hundred percent unexpected," Samantha agrees.

"For real," Rocco says with a faraway look in his eyes.

"Y'all mind if I call it a night?" Samantha asks her family. "I need to text Bo and thank him for his devious but appreciated intervention between Jules and me."

"Of course, Sweetie," her dad answers her.

"Love you, Sammie! I'm glad Jules is your friend again," Janey says sweetly.

"Me, too darlin', me too." Samantha leans over and hugs Janey.

"Rocco, you coming upstairs too, or not yet?" Samantha asks her brother.

"Yeah, wait up for me, sis." Rocco grabs his shoes and follows Samantha up the stairs.

"Hey Rocco," Samantha turns to him and continues, "Take your time with Jules. I don't want you to feel obligated in any way to get with her or whatever y'all were doing together, okay? I'm serious. Me rekindling a friendship with her will not affect you and Jules."

Rocco looks tenderly at his sister. "I appreciate that, sis, and don't worry about me. I will definitely take my time. There is no way I am jumping back into anything with Jules for a bit. Have a good sleep. See ya in the A.M." Rocco turns back toward his door, goes in, and shuts it behind him.

And my heart is telling me that it will be way sooner than later that Rocco and Jules will be hanging together. I feel like I'm floating on cloud nine; I am so happy. I guess I surely didn't realize how much stress our parting as friends had affected me. A lot, apparently. REALLY a lot. And I have only Bo to thank for his help. Wow.

This boy is becoming such a part of all of our lives. Interesting. I couldn't have predicted this summer even if I were a witch or a wizard: best friends broke apart. A new friend for Rocco, whom I adore, and a chronic disease to boot. This summer, everything changed for me!

Luckily, there is a lot of good in it, even with lots of bad.

25

SAMANTHA DROPS ONTO HER BED—HER fave spot to chill—and grabs her phone.

Samantha: *"Hola, amigo. How's the day been for y'all? I had a very interesting evening, and I know I need to thank you for this awesome event. Jules and I talked and talked for a good couple of hours. There were many tears, and surprisingly, not from me. I still have a lot of anger deeply seeded in my soul. Initially, I hesitated to let Jules in, but she looked bedraggled and sobbing, so I obviously let her in. And it's here that I am texting you to thank you sincerely for driving Jules to my house and not her own. You are very perceptive that she and I have needed each other's friendship these past months. I can honestly say that I heard Jules's explanations and found it in my heart to forgive her. Rocco and I just barely dropped her home, so thank you, Bo."*

Samantha had checked her blood sugar via her app after eating ice cream. It had been *179*—a little high, so she had made a small correction with a little insulin while in the kitchen (insulin needs to be always refrigerated).

So now, it's time to check one more time before getting into her bed, and while she awaits a text back from Bo. It's been amazing to just pull up her app and see where her blood glucose levels are.

Samantha has a tiny fridge in her room with insulin, a drawer in her dresser containing needles, her blood glucose monitor, and test strips, and a special waste container to dispose of her needles.

She gives herself her nightly injection, finishes her other nighttime stuff, and hops into her bed.

TIIINNGG

Please be Bo

Samantha grabs her phone from her side table. It's Bo!

Yasssssss

Bo: *"Hey, Samantha, sorry been downstairs hanging with the fam and my grandparents. I am glad things worked out, which is what I'd been hoping for. I know it was slightly presumptuous on my part to just drop her by your house, but as you said she was not doing well. I didn't know someone could cry that much—sheesh—also you may not know this, but you mention Jules quite a bit in your everyday conversations, ha, ha, so I took a risk."*

Samantha reads Bo's text and soaks in his words before responding.

Samantha: *"Ha, ha, I didn't realize I did that. Well, I do appreciate you taking the risk. I've needed Jules more than I realized, so thank you again! I am glad you get some time with your grandparents from Chicago!"*

Bo: *"So, are you two good now?"*

Samantha: *"We are indeed! We talked, we cried, we hugged it out, oh, and we ate chocolate almond ice cream sooo that was the best part ha, ha."*

Bo: *"So glad. I wish you a very Happy Thanksgiving. Tomorrow we're driving to my aunt's house in Waco. We will be back on Saturday, but I can text if you aren't too busy."*

Samantha: *"Sounds fab. No, it's just us this Thanksgiving, and with my T1D, we figured less stress is better this year. Well, travel safely, and I'll text ya tomorrow."*

Bo: *"Sleep well, Samantha."*

My heart pumps harder with those sweet words. Holy cannoli, I sooo like Bo. He's so kind and thoughtful, so it's no wonder Rocco is friends with him. I can now doze off with even sweeter thoughts in my heart and soul of beautiful Bo and making up with Jules....

* * *

THANKSGIVING WEEK IS CHALKED FULL OF GAMES AND FOOD. THERE ARE more games, even more food, and so much fun. Samantha texts Bo and Jules daily, and Rocco texts Bo but not Jules yet. Hopefully, when Jules comes back over again, they can rekindle their friendship. Samantha fondly recalls their summer before getting diagnosed and how great it was as the four of them hung together, swimming, lying out, and going to the movies and the mall.

Sighhhh. Things change. Often, for good, and definitely, change brings hard things like friendships and relationships broken apart and chronic diseases that are with a person for life after one single blood glucose check. I wish I could turn back the clock and go back to before I started to feel sick!! Wouldn't that BE GREAT? That would be incredible. Amazing. But, alas, life isn't like that.

Samantha openly lets out another huge sigh. She's sitting outside in her lovely backyard, just mulling over everything that has happened—she likes doing this as it helps her work through her frustrations.

It's Sunday night before going back to school after the week off for Thanksgiving and less than three weeks before her sixteenth birthday. The weather is slightly cooler now and more fall-like. Leaves in Texas are finally falling to the ground. But it's always short-lived as wintery winds usually blow off the remaining straggling leaves holding on for dear life. Samantha continues her musings.

I'm not really brooding over it all; it's more like ruminating about, well, just about everything.

What would it be like if life didn't have so many bumps on the road? I know, I know. Hard life lessons make you become a better person, but honestly, this diabetes disease has about done me in here and there. Yeah, I've been positive, for the most part, but there are some days I want to throw a large number of dishes at the wall and watch them tragically crash to the floor. I also wish I was magic sometimes.

No, I take that back. I, for real, wish I was magic and could cure myself, help others, and be for real magic, but please, that's only in silly fairytales.

Reality check Samantha! Real life sucks sometimes, and sometimes it can be for such for a long time. Friendships get destroyed for a bit and then repaired. An adorable and kind boy becomes your brother's bestie. Then that adorable and kind boy becomes your friend and slowly becomes more, and you end up becoming friends again with your own long-lost bestie because of a decision from that very same kind and adorable boy.

It's getting late, but Samantha doesn't care. She's feeling some tears start to prick her eyes, and then she lets them cascade down, down, down. Her sweatshirt is getting wet, but she doesn't care. These tears represent her and Jules being friends again. These tears represent an undying love for her family. These tears are also for her brother Rocco. Some shiny, glimmery tears are mixed in for having Bo in her life. A lot of these tears are her anger and frustration at her T1D, too, of course.

"Darlin' want to come in and have some ice cream before bed?" Samantha's mom breaks her tearful trance.

"Yeah, Momma. Give me a few minutes," Samantha says, sniffling and wiping her tears away.

"You okay, Samantha?" Her mom has obvious concern in her voice.

"I'm good, I'm okay," Samantha assures her mom.

Okay, Samantha girl, let's pull it together now. I'll let these tears come every so often, but not too much. I feel much better when I'm happy or feigning happiness, but either way, it is better for me to have these cry seshes and then pull up by big girl pants and move forward.

Samantha slides her feet into her sandals and checks her face with her phone. Her mom isn't stupid; she will see her reddened eyes and cheeks. Oh well, it is what it is for Samantha.

These moments will continue to occur occasionally, and it's okay.

26

———————

December 15

"Three more days until I'm sixteen!!" Samantha sings into her deodorant she's been clutching in her hand while looking into her bathroom mirror.

I cannot believe it's Wednesday! There are two days until Christmas break, three days until my birthday, and two and a half weeks off from school. Oh yeah, life is good!

Samantha is in her room, taking a break from studying for finals. She's got more finals on both Thursday and Friday.

Ugh. Finals week is sooooo much work! The higher-ups probably knew what they were doing for high schoolers when they did the yearly planning. Cause once Friday comes, my brain will be appropriately fried, and I won't be able to run fast enough out of the school building!

PINGGG

It's Rocco.

Rocco: *"Hey sis, you surviving?"*

Samantha: *"Uh, barely. JK, I'm okay. Almost done. How about you?"*

Rocco: *"Me too. Feel like taking a drive for a french fry run in a bit?"*

Samantha: *"Most definitely"*
Rocco: *"Cool. Say, thirty minutes?"*
Samantha: *"Setting my alarm for thirty minutes starting now!"*
BEEP BEEP BEEP BEEP

"Dang! Thirty minutes flew by!" Samantha mutters to herself. She throws on a sweatshirt and some shoes and heads toward Rocco's room, knocking lightly.

"Bro, you ready?" Samantha asks through his door.

"Yeah, give me a sec." Rocco sounds like he's huffing and puffing.

Probs grabbing a coat and shoes, too.

Sure enough, Rocco opens his door and is ready to go.

"Let's go!" Samantha smiles and follows Rocco down the stairs.

"Mom, Dad, where are you both?" Samantha calls out as she walks around the kitchen and family room.

"Oh, they're outside, Samantha. Ha, ha, I see them," Rocco says while passing Samantha and heading to the French doors to let their parents know where they are going.

"Okay, we're good to go," Rocco informs Samantha.

She grabs her crossbody, and Rocco grabs his keys. Rocco walks ahead of them both and opens the front door. Although there had been some rain earlier today, the streets were dry. Texas has deluge-like rainstorms that leave major flooding and huge puddles in the aftermath. They approach the Honda, open their doors, and slide into the car.

"Broom's or Macdonna's?" Rocco asks Samantha as he starts the car and pulls away from the curb, looking back for any cars behind him. Clear.

"Definitely, Broom's, please," Samantha responds rapidly.

"Oh crap. How's your blood sugar? I should have asked Samantha. I'm sorry." Rocco sounds very sincere and concerned.

"I'm good, Rocco. It's okay. Remember, I can check the app and set alarms to tell me if my glucose levels are too low or too high. I was just *153.*

Rocco plugs in his phone and sets up a playlist for us to listen to en route to Broom's Ice Cream and Burgers. It's only about ten minutes away from their house. Samantha has had a question on the tip of her tongue since the week of Thanksgiving. And the question is about Jules and Rocco.

"Um, Rocco, can I ask you something?" Samantha asks timidly while turning her head toward her brother.

"Yes, sis?" Rocco laughs a bit, answering in the affirmative.

"So, um, what I'd like to know is, um, have you, uh...." Samantha doesn't get to finish her sentence as she is immediately interrupted with a chortling comment from Rocco.

"Jules? Yes, actually, I wanted to tell you sooner, but I don't know. I was sort of waiting to see if I felt okay about rekindling our friendship. You can understand that sis, right?"

"Of course, Rocco, sheesh. By all means. I have been super careful not to ask Jules anything either, well, about you two, for the same reasons. I mean, it's only been a few weeks that we've been talking and hanging out again," Samantha agrees.

"Large fry for each of us?" he asks as he pulls up to make their order.

"Yes please!" Samantha answers hungrily.

Rocco pulls around to pay and get their fries, then shares more information about him and Jules. "So, I've started to text her about a week after Thanksgiving. Slowly. Carefully. Like I said, and don't say anything to her, please, but I never stopped liking her. I obviously was just as upset as you, I mean not more than you, but still pretty miffed. I knew I liked her but needed to give space between us. We've talked a lot about that Melody girl and about Jules being super dumb and scared to get diabetes—don't worry, I gave her the 411 on T1D—and being jealous of you! I mean, you share your clothes with her constantly and are always, and I mean always, nice to her. And encouraging, from what I've seen over the years. Anyway, hey, let me pull into a parking spot and continue talking. It's only 9:30ish P.M."

"Yeah, good idea," Samantha answers, shoving more fries into her mouth.

"Okay, so where was I?"

"Jules, being super dumb about me and listening to Melody."

"Right. Okay, so I can understand that we have three kids in our family, and she has five kids in her family, but like we don't care, ya know? I never think Jules is lacking in anything. I don't look at her and say that girl doesn't have nice clothes or looks unkempt."

"I totally agree." Samantha responds to Rocco between bites. "Never once have I thought that. I feel terrible that she was jealous of me. Yeah, I've got it all going on, ha, ha. Now I'm diseased!" Samantha cracks herself up with this dumb phrase that Melody has said to her multiple times.

"Okay, stop!" Rocco is laughing really hard at Samantha's comment. "That really gets me. Diseased! So dumb. You HAVE a disease. You're not diseased, and you can't give it to anyone! Gracious!"

"Yeah, that got me, but you know, if Jules was already feeling jealous or whatever, then maybe Melody feeding her all that crap just was the cherry on top for her."

"Yeah, that makes sense, and that's what Jules basically explained to me. She was just vulnerable, and she was hurt because you kept it all to yourself and to our family, but I cleared that up cause family is family."

"K, good. Appreciate that."

"Yeah, so since we're on this topic, I feel that we're—meaning Jules and me—we are making good progress, and since your sixteenth birthday is fast approaching, how fun would it be if we all four went on a double date? I mean, if Bo has talked to you about that, cause if he hasn't, then he will!" Rocco gives her a wink and laughs.

"Hey, have you been discussing me?" Samantha feigns being upset, but she's not mad one bit—she's flattered and secretly stoked!

"Only a bit." Rocco smiles.

"But, um, my b-day is literally SATURDAY?!"

"Yeah, I made that very clear to Bo, so expect a text tonight."

"Let me check my phone right now. Dang, we've been talking, and I didn't even think of it."

Samantha pulls out her phone; sure enough, she has texts from her mom, Jules, and BO!

"He asked me out! And is asking if it's okay to go as a foursome for dinner, and then we can go to the roller rink!"

Rocco can see an actual glimmer in Samantha's eyes. "Excellent. I'll ask Jules tonight, too."

"I think that is the best birthday idea! Ah, I was hoping Bo would ask me out for my b-day or at least maybe after my birthday. I am soooo happy! Do you think Mom and Dad will be cool with us four going out? Maybe we can celebrate as a family for lunch?"

"Yeah, that's a good idea, and yeah, don't even worry about it. I'm pretty sure Mom and Dad will be just fine with all of this. Speaking of, I guess we better get home!"

Rocco and Samantha continue to discuss their upcoming double date while shoveling in their delish fries, all of the deets for Saturday night. Samantha, of course, is already planning a very adorable outfit! Once Rocco parks his car, they go indoors to talk with their mom and dad about the details and plans for Samantha's birthday.

"Mom, Dad? Where are you guys? Rocco and I need to talk with you both!" Samantha is literally shouting for them in every room she enters.

"Hey sis, I see them. Back porch. Still outside." Rocco points towards their backyard.

"Oh, good! Come on!" Samantha is literally bouncing on her feet. She is so excited about Saturday night!

"Parents! Hello! Rocco and I would like to discuss an idea for, um, my b-day Saturday night, but, um…." Samantha turns to Rocco and gives him a look that says, "Hello, backup, please!"

"What Samantha is wondering, guys, is if she and I can go on a double date with Bo and Jules. We were going to go to dinner and then go to Petey's Roller Rink together. Would y'all be cool if we had a family lunch or brunch birthday celebration for Samantha earlier instead of a dinner birthday party?" Rocco looks at each of their parents and smiles, hopeful that this will be cool with them.

Mom starts to laugh and laugh! "Could you two be more stressed out looking? We're not tyrants, ya know!" She's still laughing as she's looking at both of them.

"Yeah, wow, chill out, will you two?" Dad chimes in and starts to laugh, too.

"Of course, you can go on a double date. What sixteen-year-old wants to hang with their parents on their birthday? Wait, did Bo ask you out?" Mom is literally giving her famous Cheshire cat smile as she looks at Samantha and asks this question.

"He did! Just like fifteen minutes ago!" Samantha squeals.

"Ah, sweetie, I am so glad. He's a good kid. But wait, Rocco, are you and Jules back together?" Their mom is all filled up with questions this evening.

"Uh, yeah, so I started texting her after she confessed her silly behavior to Samantha after Thanksgiving. I wasn't jumping in quickly, though. So, we're good now. Yeah, we're all going out together on Saturday. I haven't hung out with her as of yet. I just have seen her around school and texted her. Well, you know, we've talked when she's been at the house." Rocco tips his head down shyly.

Samantha comes close to him, bumps her side into him, and gives him a big smile. "We better get to bed! Two more days of blasted finals!" Samantha says goodnight to their parents, and Rocco does too.

"Love you two," her mom says sweetly.

"Ditto," says her dad.

27

Samantha and Rocco head inside to prepare for bed. Samantha will need to give herself some fast-acting insulin for her french fry run, then her long-acting to get through the night, so she heads to their kitchen first.

"I'll be up in about ten minutes," Samantha tells Rocco. He gives her a thumbs-up and heads upstairs.

She grabs her phone, quickly calculates, and gives herself her insulin. Her CGM has made such a difference for her! Just being able to see on her phone where her blood sugars are at any time has taken a huge part of her burden off of her shoulders. Samantha closes her eyes, leans against the kitchen counter, and smiles to herself:

I AM OFFICIALLY GOING OUT WITH BO!! I am freaking out with giddiness!!

Samantha puts away her insulin and heads upstairs to bed.

Two more days of school, then I'm gonna be sixteen! Hallelujah!

Samantha smiles all the way up the stairs while she sets out her outfit, washes her face, brushes her teeth, and falls into her bed in a perfectly happy place! She can barely settle down to sleep, and she's so excited for Saturday night. Of course, she'll see Bo at school, but that's not the same as going OUT with him!

She grabs her phone and puts on her lo-fi playlist, putting her headphones on, then she drifts off into the absolute best dream state she'd ever had!

"Samantha! Samantha??" Samantha is in her bathroom feeling as if she's going to hurl. She'd woken up around 5:00 A.M. feeling nauseated and found her blood sugar was 428! She hadn't been this high before, not since she was first diagnosed.

She's been lying on the bathroom floor in a ball for a while, and her head hurt badly, and she couldn't answer her mom for fear of hurling.

She needed more insulin. STAT.

Apparently, eating French fries late at night wasn't the best idea. Ugh. Who knew?

Samantha hears her mom ascending the staircase and walking down the hallway to Samantha's room.

"Samantha? Where are you, sweetie? Are you okay?"

"Mm," Samantha moans.

"Good grief! Samantha, what in the world?" Her mom grabs her phone and opens the app to check Samantha's blood sugar: *485*.

"Oh, my stars. Okay, hold on! Rocco!! Rocco??!!"

"Mom, I'm in the kitchen. What's wrong?" Rocco could hear the sense of urgency in his mom's voice.

"Grab a syringe and the fast-acting insulin quickly, please, and three water bottles," she asks with firmness in her voice.

"Of course," Rocco shouted back.

Janey wakes up in the chaos, comes into Samantha's room, and lays on her bed, waiting for her mom. Their dad is already at work.

It's about 7:30 A.M., and high school starts at 8:15. It might not be enough time to get Samantha's blood sugar down in time to get to school and feel okay at the same time. Rocco pops his head into Samantha's bathroom.

"What's happened?" He sounds nervous.

"It's okay. Everyone, keep calm. Hand me the syringe and insulin, please, dear. Samantha's blood sugar is almost 500," their mom answers. "Samantha felt too ill to get her insulin and syringe out. She feels hurly and very thirsty."

"Oh, crud. Sorry, Samantha." Rocco looks at her with deep concern and care in his eyes.

Their mom fills the syringe and slowly gives Samantha some insulin. As when Samantha was first diagnosed, bringing the high blood sugar number down slowly is key so as not to get low too quickly.

"Rocco, help me get Samantha in her bed, please." Rocco and her mom carefully lift Samantha off the bathroom floor and put their hands under her arms, and she walks, supported by them, to her bed. Janey quickly moves herself to Samantha's fuzzy chair in the corner of the room.

"I'll call the school. How many finals do you have today?" her mom asks Samantha.

"Just two, Mom, but I **can't** miss them!" Samantha feels tears gathering in the corners of her eyes. Being too high or too low really jacks up the emotions when you've got TD1.

"Well, you're going to have to see if you can make them up tomorrow. We can't play around with your health." Her mom had on THAT kind of face—the don't-argue-I've-got-your-back-but-you're-staying-put look—so Samantha let it go.

"Please try sipping water, too. It may take a few hours for your blood sugar to come down, so get as comfy as possible." Samantha nods, grabs a water bottle, and slowly sips the water.

"Rocco, please take Janey to Claire's house. I texted Lana, and she'll take her to school today."

"Sure Mom, of course. Hang in, sis, I'll test ya later, K?"

Samantha can only nod. Tears have been trickling down her face as Rocco and her mom helped her into her bed a little bit ago.

"Come on Janey! Let's go by McDonald's before I take you to Claire's house, okay?"

"Oh, Janey," Mom adds. "Please just buy lunch today, okay?"

"Sure, Momma," Janey says softly. She hugs her mom and Samantha and then goes out to get herself dressed for the day.

"I'm sorry, Mom!" Samantha says softly, "These lows and highs really suck!" Samantha tells her mom, who's now sitting on the edge of her bed handing her a tissue from the box on her bedside table. Samantha wipes away her tears. She really wasn't trying to cry, but she still felt so sick and so sad!

"You never, ever need to apologize! It's not anything to be sorry for. We learn, and we move on as best as we can." Her mom takes Samantha's hand and holds it.

"The fries were too much before bed, and I was so happy and didn't really care, ya know?" Samantha sniffs and takes another tissue to blow her nose.

"I know, sweet girl. Your blood sugar number will come down, and before you know it, you'll feel back to normal in a few hours." Her mom's face got serious. "I am sorry, Samantha. These are the times when I wish I could just wave a magic wand and wish it all away." Her throat catches, and Samantha squeezes her hand. They stay like this for a few minutes.

"Okay, let me go and call the school. Also, we will need a system when you wake up like this again. You know you can just ask Siri to call Dad or me? We would never care what time it is! You know that, right?"

"Yeah, I just thought I wasn't feeling well, and I surely didn't actually equate how I was feeling with high blood sugar. Next time, I will, for sure." Samantha gives her mom a warm smile.

Her mom gets up and heads toward Samantha's door to get her cell phone in the kitchen so she can call the high school. "Do you think you can rest? I'll check your blood sugar number every thirty minutes to ensure it's coming down slowly and steadily." She smiles at Samantha.

"Yeah, I feel pretty tired and still very crappy," Samantha says as she adjusts herself in her bed.

"Okay, sweetie, I'll return in a bit."

Samantha sips some more water and closes her eyes. A few more tears squeak from her now-closed eyes as Samantha tries to relax and perhaps fall asleep.

"Samantha? Wake up, sweetie. It's mom." Samantha's mom is gently rubbing Samantha's shoulder to help her wake up.

"Mom? What time is it?"

"It's almost 2 o'clock!"

"What the heck?"

"And you'll be happy to know your blood sugar is 179!"

"Oh, bless up!!"

"Okay, want to come and eat? Do you feel like it now?"

"Yeah, sure. Let me answer a few texts, and I'll come down. Thanks, Mom."

"Of course."

Samantha smiles to herself as her mom exits her room. She grabs her phone. There are forty messages! It takes her about twenty minutes to respond to everyone who'd texted her. Among the messages were those from her dad, Bo, Rocco, and Jules. Samantha gets a pit in her stomach, thinking Bo might not want to date a girl with days like today.

Sighhh. Bo was so sweet and said he missed me, and that Rocco had filled him in on what had happened with my blood sugar this morning. He wished me well and said he'd text me again later on. Oh, and that the art final was a breeze and that I'll do just fine on it. I sincerely hope he doesn't think I'm a broken person. I can't help but think I feel broken having this disease, so why would anyone want to deal with a person who is anything but normal? I know, I know, I'm being dramatic. Bo isn't even like this, but today was A LOT for me. A LOT.

Samantha answers a few more texts, then grabs her slides and sweatshirt and heads downstairs. She felt literally starved now! She would love anything available to eat—she isn't feeling the least bit picky! Sweet smells hit her nose as Samantha descends the stairs and enters the kitchen.

"Hey, sweetie. I've got grilled cheese sandwiches and tomato basil soup. Does that sound okay?"

"Sounds fabulous, Mom. Thank you very much." Samantha sits at their large island, and her mom brings her food. Samantha eats voraciously and asks for another grilled cheese sandwich.

"You poor thing, you were starved!!" her mom says as she pulls out the cheddar cheese block and the cheese grater.

"Thanks, Mom, you're the best! I guess I was a little hungry, huh?"

They both laugh. Samantha cleans up her lunch mess, loads the dishwasher, gives herself her insulin shot, and tells her mom she's going to shower and get on studying for tomorrow.

"Okay, sweetie. Hang in there! One more day!" Mom smiles as she washes, pans, and loads more dishes. Samantha comes over and gives her mom a big hug.

"Love you, Mom."

"Love you, back."

28

Saturday, December 18—Samantha Turns Sixteen Today!

The sun peaks through the sides of Samantha's drapes. Her eyes slowly open as she realizes that today is HER SIXTEENTH BIRTHDAY!

I made it!! It's not only Saturday, but it's my birthday! I can't believe I'm sixteen. I literally thought this day would never come since I met Bo this summer! Argh. It's been a long seven months, that is for sure. And now, it's THE DAY.

Samantha jumps out of bed, makes it, tidies her room, showers, and gets dressed for their family brunch. It's 10:12 A.M. They're going to leave around 10:30, so yay, she is all ready to go. There's only one small downer—she doesn't have her license yet. She had to put off taking driver's ed this past semester until she got better acclimated to her diabetes.

One of the very important things to be aware of is that driving with T1D differs from driving with non-type 1 diabetics. Before driving, those with T1D had to be aware of their blood sugar, how far they'd be driving, and if there was a potential to have a low or high blood sugar issue, so it's a whole thing. Samantha's mom signed her up for after-school and Saturdays to take driver's ed in the spring, so that will be great. And ever since the high blood sugar fiasco the other day, both her mom and she now have the CGM app on their phone, and they're all linked, and some alarms will go off if Samantha goes too low or too high. She'd really only had a lot of lows and hardly any highs and Samantha was able to handle those herself, but this last situation was a doozy and put all of them on edge, so they came together and talked on Friday and got a new plan in place. They'd remembered that concept while training, but now they'd use it!

Samantha did a once-over check on herself in her bedroom mirror. She was wearing a favorite light pink sweatshirt, her favorite Anthro jeans, her stacked Converse pink high tops, and she had straightened her hair. She'd change before their date tonight but felt cute and happy for family brunch.

Samantha applied her favorite matte lipstick and went out her door, hearing bustling and noise downstairs. As she entered the kitchen, her beautiful family was waiting for her. They yelled, "Happy Birthday!" unanimously and gave her lots of hugs and cheek kisses.

"You guys, it looks so cute downstairs! Thank you!" Everyone had decorated the downstairs in various shades of pink for Samantha. There were steamers, balloons, pink banners... the works! It was perfectly festive!

"Are we ready, everyone?" Samantha burst out the words happily!

All of them agree with a resounding YES. They'll be going to The Starburst Cafe, a local restaurant that was well known for its specialty pancakes. They'd discussed eating and then coming home to open gifts. Usually, Samantha is all about gifts, but things have changed since summer. Her heart has changed—she values her family more than her friends and is grateful for her life more than she'd ever even thought of in her young life. Now, she really doesn't care about WHAT she gets today. She is simply grateful to BE with these beautiful people and, of course, so stoked for the foursome to go out again! It had been months due to the whole, you know, chronic disease, the sitch with Jules, and so forth.

Brunch is fabulous, and Samantha is careful about what she eats, being careful to calculate it properly, giving herself enough insulin in the bathroom at the restaurant. Yeah, she'd become braver and learned that this was her life now, so either she embraced it or fought it. If Samantha fought it, according to Dr. Swaneyard, T1D would win, so Samantha had been working very hard to be very precise—except for the french fry incident—but that's part of learning to live with T1D. Also, she wants to keep a careful watch on her blood sugar numbers to not mess things up for later that night.

They finish their food and head toward home for the present time! It's already almost 1:00 P.M., and she and Rocco needed to be ready by 4:30 because the skating rink was closed to the general public by 7:00, and then the place has reserved party time. They'd all get dinner after, they'd decided.

The weather is decent for December, allowing everyone to dress less wintry for tonight. Also, Christmas is in a week, but all Samantha can think of is turning sixteen and going out with Bo.

No one can blame her for that!

Once home, present time begins. Janey had made Samantha the cutest key chain with pony beads. Later, Samantha would put it in her backpack. From Rocco, she got movie gift certificates!

"Thank you both. Oh, how you know your sister well!" Samantha stands up from the family room couch to hug them both. Next comes the parental gifts. Samantha got a mani and a pedi day gift card to go with her mom.

"Sweet, Mom! Love this, and boy, do I need it!" Samantha puts out her hands dramatically to show everyone her hands and fingernails. Everyone laughs. She also got a refill on her fave perfume. She'd run out a few weeks ago and was desperate to get more.

"Thanks, Mom and Dad. You know I love this perfume!" Samantha grins with elation. There were two more tiny gifts left. Samantha goes to grab the bulky one, but her dad says to open the other one first.

"Oh, yes!" It's a gift card to her favorite clothing store in the mall. "You know I can't wait to use this! Thank you, beautiful parents," Samantha says in a sing-songy voice.

"One more gift for you," her dad said, scooping it up and giving it to Samantha.

"Thanks, Daddio!" Samantha tears the package open to reveal a key fob.

Wait, it's a CAR KEY FOB!!

"Holy, what? Guys? What? You didn't get me a car, did you?'" Samantha's eyes are huge and full of excitement.

"I'm not sure. What do you think, Annie? Should we go outside and see?" Her dad chuckles as he says this.

"Why not, Ben? It sounds like it may be fun!" Her mom is also giggling.

Everyone gets up, and Samantha runs to the front door, flings it open, and runs outside. There in the driveway was a lovely, used, black Honda! She clicks the key fob, and the car beeps. She turns with a wholehearted smile as she sees her family gathered on the front porch.

"Oh, my goodness!" Samantha runs to the car, opens the driver's side door, and climbs in. It smelled delightful, clean, and new. She looks at the odometer—45,000 miles. Sweet! Her dad is a ninja car purchaser! She opens the door and gets out, running over to her parents and gathering them both in a huge hug.

"You guys, I don't even deserve this. I don't even know how to thank you enough for this car!" Samantha is grinning ear to ear! She's so joyful and overwhelmed by her gifts that she keeps hugging her parents.

"We know this has been a tough few months, and we know you'd hoped to have your license by today, so we thought we'd get you a car now as you begin your driver's ed training. Then, you can get used to driving your own car," her mom explains.

Samantha's eyes are watery. "Thank you both. Thank you all! I'm gonna go call Jules and tell her!"

Samantha ran inside and upstairs. She immediately called Jules and told her all the details of her birthday gift. "You and I get to go cruising in a car—together—just us, as soon as I get my license, of course! And we can go shopping together—just us!!"

Jules and Samantha giggle as Samantha goes on and on. As soon as she hangs up the phone, it's time to get ready to go!

She packs her tiny backpack purse filled with juice pouches and syringes, insulin, test strips, and a blood glucose monitor in case her CGM falls out or who knows. She never knew she'd have this in her life—to have to be overly prepared for what-ifs with her T1D! But she sure was here now.

Now, to get ready!

Samantha put on her already worn jeans with holes in the knees and an adorable pink floral blouse. She would wear her New Balance shoes—pink, of course—and she'd decided earlier to just pull her long hair up into a high ponytail and add a soft pink ribbon.

Rocco: *"U ready sis?"*

Samantha: *"Totes. Give me two more minutes."*

Rocco: *"Kk, meet you downstairs."*

Samantha: *"Cool."*

Samantha got her tiny backpack, swiped on more of her magic lipstick, and bounced like a little kid out of her bedroom and down the stairs. Her parents and Janey would take Janey to a movie tonight since Rocco and Samantha would be out all evening. Their curfew would be midnight since it was Sunday tomorrow, which was plenty of time to have the bestest b-day celebration with her bestie, her fave bro, and Bo!

"You guys have so much fun at the movies, okay? We will send pics throughout the night!" Samantha says as she walks over to hug her parents and Janey.

"You know I'm going to say the trite but true phrase as you go on your first date: MAKE GOOD CHOICES!" Her mom laughs as she says this, but Rocco and Samantha know she is dead serious!

"See ya, guys," Rocco says. "We will be home before midnight."

"Bye!" Her mom, dad, and Janey say together.

Rocco opens the front door and gestures to Samantha to go through it.

"Thank you!" Samantha feels like her insides are full of a thousand butterflies in her stomach, and her brain is so full of happy thoughts that she can barely contain them!

Rocco and Samantha get into the car. Samantha will ride in the front passenger seat until they pick up Jules, then she will move to the backseat, and Bo will be with her.

29

THEY ARRIVE at Jules's in a hop and a skip since she lives so close to them. Rocco walks up to get Jules.

Ahh, She looks beautiful!! I am thrilled for her and for Rocco, For real.

Rocco lets Jules in on the passenger front side. She gets in and immediately turns to Samantha.

"Happy birthday, Samantha!" she says, handing Samantha a gift.

"Ah, thanks, Jules, but you know you never have to get me anything! I'm just glad we're friends." They squeeze each other's hands.

"Open it!" Jules squeals as Rocco starts the car and drives toward Bo's house. He lives a good fifteen minutes away. Rocco has already queued up excellent birthday tunes, so they are rocking out.

"Okay, okay!" Samantha says cheerfully. She unwraps the gift and carefully peels back the paper. Inside is an amazing collage of pictures of her and Jules over the past five years.

"Oh, Jules, it's so incredible! Thank you!" Samantha and Jules squeeze hands again.

"Samantha, no tears! This is a happy day!" Rocco laughs, saying that Samantha has experienced more than enough of an emotional rollercoaster since July 17th.

"You're really cute, bro, really cute!" Samantha says sarcastically.

"Isn't he though?" Jules says, fluttering her eyelashes at Rocco.

"Okay, you two, none of that. It's too early in the night to begin that stuff!" But Samantha knows how they feel about each other, and she's happy. She sees Rocco take Jules's hand in his and squeeze it.

It's so sweet.

Samantha is hoping Bo will hold *her* hand tonight. They'd come close over the past month, she could tell. However, Samantha knew Bo was cautious and did not want to speed anything up before Samantha's sixteenth birthday. Samantha is seriously hoping tonight she'll get to hold hands and get a goodnight kiss!

A girl can dream!!

"I'll go and get Bo, guys," Samantha says, beaming as she exits the car. She walks up Bo's front pathway to his front door. She's so nervous!

Okay, chill out, Samantha. This is Bo. He's the nicest and most adorable guy. He likes you, and you like him, so yeah, I'm good. So... chill out!!

Samantha takes a deep breath and knocks on Bo's front door. Bo's mom, Lana, opens it.

"Happy birthday, Samantha! Come on in! Bo is still fixing his hair. But don't tell him I told you that." She winks at Samantha and smiles.

Samantha walked into their beautiful, open, and well-lit house. Claire runs over and hugs Samantha.

"Happy birthday, Samantha!" Claire says sweetly.

"Thank you, sweet girl. Thank you."

Just then, Bo comes walking down the staircase.

Samantha's heart literally jumps inside of her chest!

Did he get hotter overnight? Oh, my stars... be still my heart. Holy moly. This boy makes me crazy happy, and wow. He's so hot! And sweet to boot!

"Hey, Bo," Samantha says quietly.

"Hey Samantha, and happy birthday! Sorry that on our first date, YOU'RE picking me up instead of vice versa! I apologize!" He gives Samantha a beautiful smile.

"Bo, you know I don't even care!" Samantha snaps herself out of yet another *BO IS SO HOT* reverie! "Come on, let's go!" She says, and she grabs Bo's hand. "Bye, Ms. Lana!"

"Bye, Samantha! Have so much fun!"

"Bye, Mom. Bye Claire!"

"Bye, guys!" they hear Claire say as they close the door and walk to the car, walking close to each other.

Samantha's arm sizzles with electric love feels! She instantly wonders if Bo felt the same love sizzles. She really didn't know what else to call them! Maybe one day she'll ask him!

* * *

"Um, we already picked up Jules, so we're ready for roller skating. I'm pretty excited, not gonna lie." Samantha's beautiful shiny hair glistens in the Moonlight, and Bo notices.

This girl makes me crazy! She's so gorgeous! Bo thought to himself. *Dang!*

He opens the door on the side he hopes Samantha was sitting on, and Samantha climbs in. Then, he went to the other side.

"Let's get this party started!" Rocco says as Samantha and Bo are buckling their seatbelts. They all laugh.

"It's good to be back together, you guys. Don't you agree?" Bo asks.

* * *

The other three fully agreed with the 'heck yeses' and 'about times.' Samantha is so glad that this had all worked out. It had been touch-and-go for a long while, and she wasn't sure what would happen with the Jules sitch, so she is very grateful it all worked out. Samantha isn't under any false impression—she knows it could have turned out very differently.

"Here we are!" Rocco announces, parking the car and going around to let Jules out. Bo does the same, and they all begin their comfortable banter and conversation, just like last summer.

30

THE ROLLER RINK isn't as packed as Samantha had thought, but they chose to come earlier, too, just in case. All four of them were decent skaters, which made it super fun.

They skated for a good hour when they all decided it was time for some beverages. They were so sweaty from the amazing tunes and skating they'd just done! Luckily for Samantha, there's a zero-sugar soda everywhere nowadays, so she doesn't need to give herself a shot—plus, sugared soda is really hard to calculate. Samantha had barely swilled some of her soda when the slow songs montage came on. Bo smiles at her, gestures with his thumb toward the rink and, getting an approving nod from Samantha, gently took her hand and led her to the rink.

All Samantha can do was smile at Bo. The sizzle feeling is back, and it goes up and down her arm and back down again! Bo holds onto her hand for three slow songs.

This. Is. Glorious.

Samantha barely notices that Rocco and Jules have been out there too since she'd been her love bubble of joy for the entire three songs! Bo leads her off the floor, and they stand close to each other and go back to sipping their soda in silence. Rocco and Jules join them, and they begin discussing possible dinner restaurants.

"Samantha, any preference for tonight?" Bo asks her.

Samantha didn't even have to think. "Mexican food or Italian for me!"

"I'm in for either, too," Rocco and Jules agree.

"Okay then, how about Maria's Tortillas?" Bo suggests.

"Yesss! I love that place," Samantha chimes in.

"Yep, sounds good," Rocco agrees.

"Definitely," Jules adds.

The four leave the roller rink just before 7:00 P.M. and walk to Rocco's Honda. They all climb in and buckle up, and Rocco enters the address in his map app. Then, off they go. As soon as they are on the road, Bo slides his hand over and grabs Samantha's.

Let the sizzle feeling begin again.

She turns her head toward Bo, smiles at him, and squeezes his hand. Samantha notices that Rocco had taken Jules's hand again, too.

Who knew that since last summer, so much would change in my life? I certainly didn't have a clue that all of this would be coming to pass, but most of all, I am so grateful that Bo moved to Texas!

The group make their way to Maria's Tortillas for dinner. Bo holds Samantha's hand and pulls her out of the car. They walk hand-in-hand to the restaurant, as do Rocco and Jules. While looking at their menus and ordering the food, Samantha is surprised when Bo pulls a small package out of his pocket and gives it to her.

"Happy Birthday, Samantha," Bo says softly to her.

Samantha smiles and takes the gift. "Bo, you didn't have to get me anything! You already paid for roller skating, and now you're paying for dinner. I seriously appreciate your kindness so much," she says.

Bo looks at Samantha and says, "Of course, I was going to get you a gift. You only turn sixteen once, don't you?" He gives her his beautiful smile, which melts Samantha's heart.

Bo then says, "Open it up, Samantha!"

She rips off the paper and finds a beautiful bracelet—the stretchy kind with beads, but this one had every hue of pink in it.

"Oh, I love this bracelet!" Before she knows it, she leans over and kisses Bo on the cheek. Then she immediately pulls back and turns so many shades of red! Leave it to Bo, though, to make the situation less embarrassing. He leans over and kisses her back on the cheek.

"You're welcome, Samantha. Happy sixteenth birthday."

Meanwhile, across the table, Rocco and Jules have been doing their own thing, talking and being googly-eyed to each other, so they were oblivious to Bo and Samantha, which is just as well with Samantha.

The food finally comes! Everyone is starving, so they all dig into their food, eating and having a continuous, easy, and enjoyable conversation between them. Every so often, Samantha just turns and looks at Bo and thinks to herself:

I *am on a date! I am on a date with this absolutely adorable human being. How did I get so lucky?*

Then she'd catch herself being a weird starer at Bo and would turn away quickly! The four of them went all out with their ordering since it was Samantha's birthday, and they ordered dessert and fantasy drinks. They had the absolute best time at dinner! Samantha didn't want this night ever to end, but, unfortunately, the time was passing rapidly, and by the time they'd finished, it was around 11:15 P.M.—time to wrap it up and take everybody home.

Rocco and Jules walked hand-in-hand to his car. Bo and Samantha also walked hand-in-hand, and at this point, all Samantha could think of was there was no way she could get a kiss goodnight because they were dropping Bo off first! Samantha felt slightly disappointed but realized it was not a big deal. She and Bo had held hands the entire night. He still had her hand in his while driving home in the car.

The music was on, the sizzling feeling was going between her hand and his hands, and it was warm—she was just giddy with happiness. Every so often, she gazes at her birthday bracelet on her left hand and smile at herself at how thoughtful and kind BO is. How hot BO is. But most of all, he is kind. And fun.

Samantha loves that Rocco and Bo are friends, that she and Jules are friends, and that it's been the absolute best to all be friends since summer, well, except for the incident with Jules, but that's over and done.

Unbeknownst to Samantha, Bo had secretly texted Rocco during dinner to ask if he could drop Samantha and Bo off at Bo's house. Then, Bo would take Samantha home. So, when they get to Bo's house, Samantha is ready to get out of the car and walk Bo up to his house, which she did.

But Bo surprises her by saying, "Hey, why don't I just take you home? Would that be okay?

He's asking me if that would be okay. It would be more than okay. In fact, it would be the best thing ever because then Bo would be taking me home to my house.

She texts Rocco and Jules.

Samantha: *"Thanks for an awesome night. Bo says he'll give me a ride home."*

To which both of them give her heart-eyed emoji. Bo takes Samantha's hand and opens his front door, and they walk inside.

"Hey, Mom. Hey, Dad," Bo says. "I'm just going to run Samantha home. Is that okay with you guys?

"Hey kids, how was the night? Ms. Lana asks.

"It was wonderfully fun," Samantha retorts. "The roller rink was so great, and then we ate at Maria Tortillas for dinner. And look at the bracelet that Bo got for me!"

Ms. Lana gets up, walks to Samantha, and looks at it. "Oh, Bo, you did a nice job on this gift for Samantha. I love it."

BO says, "Thanks for the vote of confidence, Mom. I do know how to pick out gifts."

Ms. Lana laughs and says, "I know, sweetie, I know! Just giving you a hard time!"

Bo grabs his keys and reaches for Samantha's hand as they walk out the front door, which he shuts behind them. They walk slowly to the curb to get to Bo's car. He opens the passenger side door and lets Samantha in, then he walks around, lets himself in, turns on the car and immediately turns on the music.

He then turns to her. "Samantha, I've been waiting a really long time to be able to take you out. I wanted you to know that I probably would've held your hand and kissed you sooner, but I wanted to respect your family's role and wait until you were sixteen.

Samantha turns to look at Bo. "I really appreciate that, Bo. I didn't really think you would stick around, but you proved to me that you were not like any other guy I've met so far. And I am glad you're friends with my brother Rocco. And I appreciate you being patient and putting up with, well, our family rule and my disease. I've been a little nervous thinking that perhaps you wouldn't want to hang with a girl who's basically broken," she says quietly and nervously.

But Bo takes her hand and says, "Samantha, I don't care what you have. I just care about you. I like you. You're fun. You're kind. You're a very strong and brave person because of all that you've gone through since your diagnosis. And I admire you for this. Actually, I feel exactly the opposite of that. I'm in awe and impressed with you, and I'm grateful you would hang out with me."

She smiles sweetly and says, "The feeling is mutual. You're the best. You're so much fun to hang out with, and I love that we're in art class together. Plus, I couldn't ask for a better thing than for you and me to be friends for a while and then for us to like each other along the way. It's been really awesome for me, especially through everything I've been going through."

"Well, that's good because I feel the same way," he says. "You're amazing, and I look forward to getting to know you even more." He softly takes her hand and, turning the car away from the curb, starts toward Samantha's house, steering with the other hand. They have a nice conversation while listening to music and chatting pleasantly about this and that until they get to Samantha's house.

He turns off the car and goes around to let Samantha out. He takes her hand, helps her out of the car, and holds onto it as he walks her to the front door. "Samantha, um, I want to make sure it's okay that I ask if I can kiss you tonight. As I said previously. I would've kissed you sooner. But I wanted to be respectful, and I also wanted to have a good friendship between us. But if you let me, I'd like to give you a birthday kiss goodnight."

Obviously, Samantha doesn't even have to respond, but she does anyway. "I thought you'd never ask!"

And that's when he leans down, gently puts his lips on her lips, and gives her the softest and sweetest kiss ever. Samantha closes her eyes for the duration of the kiss, so when Bo pulls away, she quickly opens her eyes and follows suit.

They look into each other's eyes, and then they both say goodbye. She watches him walk down the pathway from her front door to his car.

Samantha goes into her house, delirious with happiness. She peeks out the side window and watches him enter his car and drive away. Then, as if in a movie, Samantha turns around, leans against the closed door, and gives a dramatic, delightful sigh.

Although the characters in this story are fictional, every part about T1D is true. I would like to share four true accounts of children diagnosed with T1D. The first is from me, followed by my sister's story and two friends whose children were diagnosed last summer. (All names are changed to protect their privacy.)

* * *

Story #1:

July 17, 1998, was six months after my son Jake had been seriously ill, along with his big sister, with a nasty virus that then triggered a gene that he had in his body, predisposing him to get T1D. By July, Jake was whiny (and this was NOT his personality—he was the sweetest kiddo), losing weight, and always hungry and thirsty. He'd also been peeing out of his diapers for the past few weeks!

It took me one month, after looking at Jake's symptoms, to take Jake to our pediatrician. Within five minutes, the nurse checked Jake's urine to see if he had ketones in his urine—which he did—meaning that he had a chronic disease! (They did urine tests in these days). From there, we were to go by ambulance to Primary Children's

Hospital (we lived in Salt Lake City at the time) to have Jake's blood sugar tested and for us to learn how to care for Jake and his T1D.

His blood sugar was 690!! He was well on his way to going into a diabetic coma. He looks so sickly when I looked back at the pictures from that weekend. By the end of the weekend (we'd gone in on Friday evening and left on Sunday), he was back to his sweet self and was running all over the hospital! From there, we gave Jake shots in his tiny arms for two and a half years and did blood checks six to eight times per day.

He finally got an insulin pump from Minimed by age four and a half, which SAVED Jake and us! Jake could finally go to birthday parties and eat much more freely, and we could bolus for his food (give him a push of fast-acting insulin).

It's been almost twenty-seven years since that day at 4:00 P.M. when our lives changed forever, especially Jake's. He's never known anything else but living with diabetes since he was so young when he was first diagnosed—moms don't forget these dates—and I am proud to say that Jake has done a fabulous job maintaining and living with his T1D.

I am so happy to share this story about Samantha, aka, Jake. :)

* * *

Story #2:

July 30, 202, Liam's diagnosed with Type 1 diabetes. It was a pretty weird year for us. In the spring of 2021, our son Liam made some very rash, scary decisions without a lot of thought behind them. We were worried about him, so we took him to a counselor. She diagnosed him with possible bipolar disorder. By mid-summer, we had started him on some mood-stabilizing medication. It was his first experience with

any mental health medication. The side effects of the medication were pretty extreme: muscle pain, frequent urination, thirst, and stomach pain.

So, we had no idea he was actually experiencing severe diabetic ketoacidosis. He was heavily involved in the marching band at the time and was attending a summer band camp. He would come home so exhausted that he just lay down and couldn't move till the next morning. I was getting worried but figured it would take a month for him to get used to the new medicine he was taking.

Over two weeks, he lost a noticeable amount of weight. I couldn't believe the effects of the medication he was on and was extremely worried. T1D was the furthest thing from my mind at that moment. We decided as a family to go to Glenwood Springs for the weekend before the kids had more band camp and then head back to school. When we got there, we headed to a nice restaurant. Liam could barely touch his food and looked so sickly that we packed his food and started to head back to our car. Liam threw up and could scarcely stand.

I finally decided enough was enough and headed into the hospital in Glenwood Springs. The doctor did all sorts of tests on him. Jeff took my other two kids back to the hotel. The doctor then told me that Liam's blood sugar was 739. I had absolutely no idea what in the world that meant. He said to me that he probably has diabetes. After a few swirly minutes, I clarified with the doctor—wait, does this mean he might have diabetes, or is it for sure diabetic? He said yes, he is absolutely type 1 diabetic. I was so scared. I had no idea what that meant for us. They tried all night to get his blood sugars down slowly. They then wanted us to head up to Denver. I told them I would rather go to Primary Children's in Utah, where I had family support. Jeff had to head back to Montrose for an important work meeting, so the kids and I headed to Utah.

I had never done a shot before or knew anything about T1D except what I had seen with my nephew, and since I was a teenager when my nephew was first diagnosed, I was pretty oblivious to it all. They didn't send us with any insulin or anything (which, looking back, I realize how dangerous that was). Liam was pretty out of it but was starting to feel a little better.

By the time we made it to Utah, my sister or parents—I can't remember—were headed to Primary Children's to grab my other two children, but it was pretty late. Liam and I headed in to check-in. I was so confused and overwhelmed that I started to lose it when I was talking to the front office. They got us settled in the juvenile diabetic wing in a room. They kept asking me if they sent Liam with any insulin from the Glenwood hospital. I told them no, and they were very shocked. Three different people kept asking me the same thing.

They hooked Liam up to IVs and started giving him insulin. I can't fully remember, but I think his blood sugar was 300 to 500 by that time. Jeff got back up to Utah a day later, and we started our week's stay at the hospital with Liam, which included diabetic training for us and Liam. We watched videos, read materials, and met with so many different medical professionals—dietitians, endocrinologists, nurses, social workers, etc. We started to learn how to count carbs and account for insulin to help the carbs get absorbed into Liam's cells.

Liam was a champ. He gave himself shots and did a fantastic job. At the week's end, we were discharged and sent home. To say we were overwhelmed with it all was an understatement. I was horrified. How would Liam be able to do everything and juggle diabetes? It was so stressful. I kept telling Liam that his cousin Ian had a normal life and could do anything he wanted, and that diabetes would not prevent him from doing anything he wanted. Inside, I was still in shock that this was the moment Liam's life would change forever!

Story #3:

Ella was diagnosed with type-1 diabetes (T1D) on Saturday, June 1, 2024 (at age 11). She had complained of an upset stomach a few days earlier in the week but felt fine otherwise. Then Ella vomited late Thursday night and Friday morning, so at first, we thought maybe she had a stomach bug or something. She didn't have a fever or other symptoms, but she felt weak and tired.

We tried to keep her hydrated and let her rest, but she kept getting worse. She became very weak and disoriented and started having labored breathing on Friday night, which was very concerning and seemed inconsistent with a stomach virus or flu. We decided to wait and see if she was doing any better in the morning, but her labored breathing continued, and she had become so weak and disoriented that she needed help to walk or stand. And she said a few times that she couldn't see! At that point, we knew something was wrong, but we had no idea what it could be.

It was now Saturday morning, and Rob was gone with Liam at a day camp, so I left my other kiddos with my eldest and took Ella to urgent care. She was so weak at this point that I had to help her to the car, and I asked for a wheelchair for her when I got to urgent care. They took her back to a room immediately upon seeing her and must have had a good idea of what was wrong based on her presentation, because the first thing they did was check her blood glucose.

The doctor was very abrupt in telling me that her glucose was 560 (very high! Normal is between 80-120) and that she most likely had T1D. I was shocked! We don't have any history of diabetes in our family, and I had no idea what the symptoms she was experiencing could be.

They gave her an IV and started giving her an insulin drip to lower her blood sugar levels slowly (it can be dangerous to let them drop back down too quickly) and contacted Children's Health in Plano to have her transferred there by ambulance. She was still very disoriented while we were waiting for the ambulance and kept asking for water, but they could only give her ice. At this point, it was the first time I noticed any signs of excessive thirst, which apparently is a common diabetes symptom.

I followed the ambulance to the children's hospital about 20 minutes away and met them in the hospital room right after Ella had arrived. Two doctors were there to greet me and tell me everything that was going on. Then, they started asking me questions about the symptoms Ella was experiencing. They asked if she had any excessive thirst, frequent urination, or sudden weight loss, but she really hadn't had any noticeable symptoms until the day before we took her to urgent care.

They told us she was experiencing something called "diabetic ketoacidosis" (DKA), a serious and potentially life-threatening complication of diabetes that occurs when the body doesn't have enough insulin to use blood sugar for energy, so the liver breaks down fat for energy instead, producing acids called ketones. These ketones build up in the blood and make it acidic, which can harm vital organs like the brain and kidneys. (With type-1 diabetes, the pancreas doesn't make enough insulin, compared to type-2, where the pancreas still makes insulin, but the body becomes resistant to it.)

Some symptoms of DKA include:

Vomiting (yes)

Abdominal pain (yes)

Deep gasping breathing (yes)

Increased urination (yes, but only after she started vomiting and we were trying to keep her hydrated)

Weakness (definitely)

Confusion (yes, this was the scariest part for me!)

Occasionally, loss of consciousness (thankfully, she remained conscious but was very close to unconsciousness by the time we got to urgent care)

A specific "fruity" smell on the breath (I never noticed this on Ella)

Everything seemed to be happening so quickly, and I was almost in denial about her diagnosis, but at the same time, I was so thankful for modern medicine and very grateful that she was getting the treatment she needed. Ron was able to leave the day camp early and meet us at the hospital not long after we arrived.

Ella had to stay in the hospital for a few days so they could monitor her to make sure her blood sugar levels were coming down slowly. They also kept doing neurological checks on her every few hours to make sure she still had normal brain function since inflammation of the brain and other organs is a common side-effect of lowering blood sugars too quickly. They would ask her a series of questions like

"What is your name?"

"Do you know where you are?"

Who is that?" (pointing to me)

One nurse got creative with her questions and asked things like, "Who is on the Eras Tour right now? (Taylor Swift!)

Thankfully, Ella could answer the questions each time, even though she was still groggy and disoriented when awake. I felt so bad for her because she looked so tired and probably just wanted to sleep, but the nurses had to keep checking her every few hours.

In addition to the questions, they would also ask her to push her hands and feet against their hands to ensure she followed simple directions and had good muscle control. I was glad they were being so thorough and checking her so often, but I'm sure the poor girl just wanted to sleep!

She made me laugh a few times in her groggy state because she started getting annoyed at the doctors and nurses for asking her the same questions over and over. "I already told you that!" Ha, ha, that's my sassy girl!

Ella was doing a lot better by Monday. Then, she could move out of the pediatric intensive care unit into a standard hospital room, which meant her siblings could finally visit! (No kids under age five are allowed to visit the PICU—Pediatric Intensive Care Unit).

Ron and I had been receiving lots of diabetes education during Ella's stay in the hospital. Since her body doesn't make enough insulin to process sugars, she now has to track all carbohydrates she eats and give herself insulin injections based on a carb-to-insulin ratio that will be adjusted as needed based on how her body responds and whether her glucose levels stay stable or go too high or low after meals. Ron and I had also been taking turns going home in the evenings for dinner and bedtime with the kids while the other stayed in the hospital with Ella. Sara was such a big help by staying with the boys during the day, so we didn't have to worry about finding someone to watch them for us.

GOING HOME

Ella got to go home on Tuesday, June 4, after being in the hospital for three days. After lots of education and practice at the hospital, we celebrated doing her first pre-meal glucose test and insulin dose all on our own! We had the other kids watch the whole process, and Sara did a finger poke to test her glucose in solidarity.

For the first month or so after coming home, Ella had to poke her finger for glucose tests and use needles for insulin injections before every meal and at bedtime every day. Still, she was able to get a continuous glucose monitor after a few months and will be getting an insulin pump soon, which will do most of the work for her. Ella will still need to calculate carbs but won't have to do multiple daily injections anymore. She will be able to tell the pump how many carbs she's eating, and it will administer the insulin she needs. But the doctors wanted us to start with the basic methods first, so we have those to fall back on, just in case.

We are so thankful Ella is home and doing well! It was so scary having her in the hospital. She has had many moments of frustration with her diabetes but has handled it well overall. I had a good chat with her the day before we left the hospital and asked how she was doing emotionally. She cried about it for the first time. I think it wasn't really real yet, but talking about it helped it finally sink in a bit. She has had many more moments of frustration and sadness about it since then, including a very difficult first trip to the grocery store after her diagnosis. Still, she has been good about following her treatment plan and has been very mature about the whole thing, for the most part.

GIRLS CAMP

Church girl's camp was already scheduled only one week after Ella got home from the hospital! (June 10-14). At first, we were unsure about sending her, but we didn't want her to miss out on her first year of girls' camp. We left the decision up to her, and she still wanted to go, so we asked the doctors at the hospital if she could still attend. They said she could as long as there would be a nurse there who was familiar with diabetes care. Thankfully, I knew the nurse going to camp that year, and she was able to meet with us a few days before camp so we could do a run-through of Ella's specific needs and how to check her blood glucose and calculate and administer her insulin. We also sent Ella with a bin of supplies and pre-portioned snacks.

Thankfully, another girl with T1D and her mom were both attending camp that year, so they came to visit us on Sunday to meet Ella. They offered to help her calculate her carbs and help with her insulin injections before each meal. That was such a big help! That girl had had T1D for ten years, so they were very experienced and comfortable helping Ella, which made Rob and I feel so much more at ease about sending her, knowing they would be there to help her.

Ella did great on the first day of camp! But on the second day, she went on a hike, had some over-exertion afterward, and threw up. The camp nurse called and said they should send Ella home. Still, I told her the doctors had said to us that she might react differently to exercise now that she's on insulin. There were some anti-nausea meds in her medical supplies for this exact reason.

Still, Ella kept throwing up and started to have elevated ketones, which eventually led to her being taken to the nearest hospital. Ron and I found a sitter for the boys so we could drive up to Oklahoma to meet her there. Thankfully, she just needed some stronger nausea meds and IV fluids to help clear the ketones, so she didn't have to stay overnight, but she did have to miss the last few days of camp.

Hopefully, next year, she will be able to stay the whole week!

BACK TO SCHOOL

Ella started seventh grade this year and has been doing great at school since her diagnosis. We were grateful she was diagnosed over the summer so we could get the hang of things before going back to school! She got a CGM before school started, which is great because Ron and I can also see her glucose readings on our phones. She just needs to stop by the nurse before lunch every day to get her insulin injection before eating, but hopefully, soon, she will have a pump and won't need to stop by the nurse before lunch anymore.

She is in athletics this year she (wants to try out for tennis in February!), and her blood sugar levels tend to go high during exercise, so that will also be nice to have her on a pump so it can keep her levels more stable during exercise.

It has been seven months since Ella's diagnosis, and we've gotten into a good routine with everything. We made several adjustments to her carb ratio during the first few weeks home from the hospital, but she has been on the same ratios for the past few months now. We found a great food tracker app that also allows you to track diabetes info (My Net Diary), and Ron, Ella, and I can all log in to the same account to help her calculate her carbs and track anything else we want to track.

The next step is to get a pump, which we are all looking forward to! Hopefully, that will make things easier to manage and help keep Ella's levels in range.

* * *

Story #4:

SYMPTOMS: Looking back, I can see all the signs, but at the time, I just thought the symptoms were unrelated, like a growth spurt or mild case of the flu. The random babblings at night time, the frequent thirst and subsequent recurring trips to the bathroom, the occasional bed wetting (I mean, he has been potty trained since he was two and the least likely of my sons to have nighttime accidents), and the occasional rapid breathing, when all manifest together are easy to diagnose as diabetes, but not to a mom who has never had a family history or experience with diabetes.

May 14th was the day when all of those symptoms showed up together. The day started with washing his bedding from another nighttime accident, then a call around noon from the school nurse telling me he was lethargic and not acting himself. After a quick call to our pediatrician to chat about symptoms with her secretary, no response to symptom questions, an appointment scheduled for the following week, and a drive to his elementary school, I picked him up and drove him home.

He WAS acting more lethargic than I expected. Still thinking he was sick with whatever virus was going around at the time, I laid him down, tried to keep him hydrated, and rubbed garlic and oil on the bottom of his feet (the cure-all for all childhood diseases, according to my parents and their parents—my family is kind of holistic like that).

We didn't have time for Johnny to be sick! It was the second to last week of school and felt almost busier than Christmas time. There were concerts to attend, exams to take, end-of-year teacher gifts to prepare, and parties to volunteer at. My oldest had his final orchestra concert that night, May 14. So, after some rest and hydration, we went to the concert as a family. Johnny didn't have a fever and seemed a little more "like himself," so he came too.

When we arrived at the high school, the lobby was filled with parents and grandparents, all waiting for the doors to open. Johnny went and found an out-of-the-way, quieter spot in the hall and sat down with his younger brother. I was running solo that night and trying to manage my other son and our relative proximity to the auditorium doors. My husband would meet us there after work and requested we save him a seat.

Right before the doors opened, Johnny came to me and said he didn't feel well and needed a bathroom. On his way to the restroom, he vomited all over the floor. People started to scream and jump out of the way. As I ran to help him, I got odd looks from people all around me. Looks like, "Lady, why did you bring a sick kid to this event," and "Gross... your kid just puked, and it's on my shoes now."

One saint of a man ran into the restroom and offered to help my son clean up the second round of vomit, this time on the men's bathroom floor. Another man ran to find a janitor and a "slippery when wet sign." Meanwhile I frantically tried to find my other two children, and determine my husband's ETA, and then connect the two, all while feeling overwhelmed with the situation, sad that I'd miss my oldest son's performance, and mom guilt for not leaving Johnny at home resting and away from "the masses" (and their judgment).

My stars aligned. The lobby emptied. Joe arrived and took our youngest boys into the auditorium. The person helping Johnny in the bathroom opened the door and encouraged me to come into the men's room to help him while he mopped the floor and rerouted other male bathroom goers to find a different bathroom. I wiped my son's face. I felt his forehead. I thanked both men who'd rushed to our aid. Then I took Johnny to the car, and we headed home.

The ride home was silent, yet the voices in my head—the critical ones analyzing what went wrong and how it could have been prevented—were screaming at me. Looking back, why didn't I just take him to the ER right then and there? "Sweat it out" was my family's motto, which worked for most things, but tonight, we were having no luck with any of the home remedies that had always worked in the past.

When we got home, he lay down and slept. Since sleeping is when most healing of the body occurs, I just let him sleep. Jonathan arrived home with the rest of the crew, and the next hour and a half was filled with stories and video clips of the concert, bedtime routines, bedside prayers, kisses, and tuck-ins.

In the middle of my last tuck-in, my husband came in and told me that Johnny needed help and was breathing funny. I ran into the living room, where he had been sleeping on the couch, and sure enough, he had shallow and rapid breathing. This was a symptom I had seen in the past few months, but only once or twice. When isolated from other symptoms, I chalked it up to overexertion. Now that it was showing up with all these other symptoms, I knew something was seriously wrong—something that garlic and rest wouldn't fix.

Joe was headed to bed. I rushed in and told him I was taking Johnny to the ER. He questioned my decision, but after explaining my reasoning, he supported my decision. He asked if I had all the insurance cards, and to grab bag of toiletries in case we were to be kept overnight (it was 10:40 at this point... of course, we would be kept overnight), and a change of clothes should we need them.

I frantically packed and loaded the car, then went to load Johnny up. He was able to get his shoes on and walk to the car. The first fifteen minutes of our thirty-five-minute drive to the children's hospital were pretty uneventful. He casually mentioned his legs were hurting. As we got on the 121, he asked to go to the bathroom. I was feeling frantic about getting there and didn't want to try to find a roadside gas station that had an available (and somewhat clean) public bathroom at that time of night. I asked if he could wait, then started to make conversation to keep his mind off of his bodily needs.

I reached back to grab his hand, and it was cold. I started to panic. As I asked him questions and his answers didn't make sense at all. More panic. My mind went to the worst-case scenario.

I thought my son was dying.

I sent a series of silent prayers, "Dear God, please don't let him go!!! I know he's not my son—he's yours before he was ever mine, but please, let me be his mom a little while longer. And, if it can be till we're both old, then all the better. Please don't let him go!!!" And, "Dear God, whatever this may be, prepare my heart and strengthen my shoulders to bear whatever heaviness is ahead."

Between these desperate prayers, I looked at the clock and my speedometer. It felt like I couldn't get to the hospital fast enough. I was going eighty-five miles per hour and praying the cops weren't out. And if they were, maybe they could give me a police escort if they knew the rush.

"Just hang on for seven more minutes, bud." Another silent prayer. "Six minutes, and we are there, Johnny." Still speeding. "What is the one thing you look forward to this summer?" I asked.

Random non-sensical gibberish was the reply.

"Getting off the exit. Are you holding it? As soon as we get to the hospital, you can go potty, okay?" I squeezed his hand. Still cold.

Minutes seemed like hours as we finally pulled into the hospital drive. We parked in the parking structure, one of only two cars there. Hallelujah! We chose a good, non-busy night to come to the ER! The place was standing room only every other time I came.

As I opened Johnny's door, he looked like he was a few steps away from death. He didn't have the muscle strength to stand up, though he could easily walk out to the car forty minutes earlier. I grabbed a few things in my bag and had him climb on my back for a piggy-back ride. As we crossed the street to the ER entrance, I felt heaviness... and not just the heaviness I felt from carrying my almost ten-year-old. It was the heaviness of the unknown.

Did we make it in time? Would they be able to help him? What would our future hold? The latest version of the coronavirus? A new syndrome? A rare medical condition?

Not once did "incurable disease" enter my mind.

I spotted a wheelchair. I set him down on top, and we headed for the check-in counter. The nurse at the counter asked a few questions about Johnny's condition and immediately wheeled him over to two other nurses, who started to test blood pressure and weight and run other vitals. They asked me about his blood sugar and what he had eaten lately. One nurse mentioned diabetes.

We were immediately moved into a hospital room, and he was hooked up to a bunch of machines. Our room became a revolving door of nurses and doctors running blood tests and hooking up IVs. Soon, monitors flashed and beeped. I tried to find an out-of-the-way place where I could sit.

As a nurse removed Johnny's socks, I felt a slight rush of blood to my cheeks, and a hint of embarrassment crept through my body. Now, the room smelled like garlic. I ran to grab some paper towels to wipe his feet.

"Just throw the socks away," I said.

A male nurse made a joke about the garlic and referenced guacamole. He must be hungry, I thought. I was grateful that his light comment cut through some of the heaviness.

I tried to call Jonathan. It went to voicemail. He was asleep, for sure! The man probably thought this was no big deal, just a virus, and slept. After all, this was a busy week for Jonathan. His employer required mandatory overtime for all of the employees on his team. They were doing final flight testing for their customer, which meant that Joe was supposed to be "out of town" just about every day for the next ten days. It was a miracle that he had even finished work early and made it to the orchestra concert on May 14th. Now, he was sleeping. I felt grateful I could bear this burden for our family. Five months earlier, Joe was in my shoes, but with our oldest, who'd contracted a staph infection during the week of Christmas.

This time, it was my turn. I took a picture of Johnny, then texted it to my husband with the caption, "still alive... almost thriving," followed by the praying hands emoji and a heart emoji.

DIAGNOSIS: By this time, it was fairly conclusive that Johnny was dealing with DKA or Diabetic Ketoacidosis. It was the first time I had ever heard those words. In basic terms, he had a bum pancreas, and his body was unable to process sugars properly.

Slightly relieved that this was his diagnosis and not some unknown or rare disease, I took a deep breath and wondered what life would be like going forward. I mean diabetes—it's not like leprosy. I knew several kids who had diabetes growing up. I didn't know much about it. I had heard my dad talk about my uncle being pre-diabetic and changing his lifestyle, reversing his symptoms. Maybe this was the case for Johnny.

I had to force myself to stay present and not rush to Google or WebMD to find info or answers about type 1 diabetes. In this moment, I felt I needed to be strong for Johnny. If he saw me panic, then he might panic. So, I stayed present.

The doctor came every half an hour for a mental scan. She would ask Johnny a series of questions to see how his brain responded. The test had been performed several times prior, and after the last one, the ER doctor talked about moving him to a normal hospital room to be monitored.

Progress!

She came back a half hour later, and it was different this time. When she asked Johnny how old he was, which he had aced in his prior tests, he answered, "I'm not sure." Then she asked who the lady sitting next to him was (referring to me). He looked at me and said, "I don't know."

I sat there a little confused, but truthfully, it had been a long day, and I was wondering who I was myself. The doctor went out and made a phone call. When I asked what was going on, the nurses mentioned that his body was in DKA and his blood was saturated with sugar. His blood sugar was 474 (around 100 is normal). As a result, his body sent fluid to the brain, which was causing his memory to be impaired.

Nurses were trying to hydrate him and try to bring his blood sugar down but didn't want to drop his blood sugar too fast, which could bring on seizures and even death. The buzz in the ER was that we might be transferred to Children's Dallas.

Transferred? How?

Promptly, the doctor came in and said she was concerned with his latest neurology check. She feared they wouldn't have the necessary interventions if things went downhill but that Children's Dallas had all the necessary specialists and equipment. She recommended an ambulance transport. I agreed, and the transfer started.

Three EMTs entered the room and reviewed charts, tests, and monitors with the doctor and nurses. I listened in, hoping I'd catch something I may have missed. I had so many questions. That number again, 474. How high was too high, I wondered. How close to death were we? Nurses seemed pretty urgent from the moment we arrived, so it must have been high. I heard other words and acronyms, but I didn't know what they meant. What was A1C? What did it mean that he was too high to measure? It didn't sound like good news.

Cords were unplugged and transferred to mobile units. Two strong EMTs lifted Johnny to an emergency stretcher. The only female EMT of the three was gathering signatures from the doctors and making sure all T's were crossed and all I's were dotted. I clung to my coat and the clear bag they gave me to put all of Johnny's belongings in—his soiled clothes and shoes, his favorite book, and a few other minor items that I questioned even bringing.

"Can I ride in the ambulance?" I asked.

It was now 3:00 A.M. Part of me worried that if I had to follow the ambulance that I'd get stuck at a light or not be able to find him once I got to the hospital. I also worried that something might be done without my consent if I didn't ride along. Secretly, I had always wanted to ride in an ambulance. But this isn't how I had imagined that moment.

I sat up front next to the driver. He was a nice young man. He had no kids of his own. He was married and had been an EMT for several years. I wondered what kinds of cases he had seen and what kinds of stories he had from his transports. I didn't dare ask.

I did send a quick text to my husband, knowing he wouldn't get it for a few more hours. <Headed to Children's via ambulance. Johnny's failed his neurology check and needs more intervention. Doctors are 95% sure it's T1D (Type 1 Diabetes). Call me when you wake up.>

Driving down the Dallas North Tollway at 3:00 A.M. with lights and sirens was not quite how I'd imagined riding in an ambulance. It didn't feel much faster than my drive from our home to the hospital earlier that night. The tollway was mostly empty, and the drive was pretty uneventful.

I did feel more relieved than I had during that original car ride to the ER. I was on the other side of that experience now and knew that we were dealing with diabetes. My son was in good hands in the back of the ambulance, and I did feel more at peace. I didn't know what lay ahead, but I did know that many people have dealt with diabetes. It's been around for generations, and technology advances daily, so I knew we'd figure it out.

The ambulance pulled into the emergency bay, and the doors to the back opened. My sweet little guy had fallen asleep and completely missed the ambulance ride's excitement, if there had been any. I snapped a few pictures (so he'd believe me when I told him he'd ridden in an ambulance), and we rushed into the double doors of the emergency room.

The female EMT pushed past security. "We have emergency orders. This kid is really sick and needs to be moved to a room stat! Here are the orders. This is his mom. She's coming with us and will fill out admittance paperwork later."

At that moment, I knew I'd made the right decision to ride in the ambulance. I also felt the full weight of the experience and diagnosis hit my shoulders when she talked about how sick Johnny was, and I saw the security guards step aside without question.

It was now 4:00 A.M. I had been awake for almost a full twenty-four hours and was only running on five to six hours of sleep from the previous night. My brain felt tired.

Once Johnny was settled into his new room and the transfer of information had been done, I felt like I couldn't finally lay down and rest. A nurse handed me a bag with some toiletries, probably packed and donated by volunteers, and asked me to follow her on a quick tour of the floor. She showed me where I could get a towel and some bedding, pointed me toward the bathrooms with showers, and showed me how the ice machine and coffee/tea station worked.

I was too tired to shower, and I didn't have clothes to change into. They were in my grab bag in my van and had been left there when the emergency transport chaos began.

It was now 5:00 A.M. Joe would surely be up in the next hour and a half. But he was supposed to be doing mandatory overtime. How would our kids get to school?

I opened my phone and sent another text. <We made it to Dallas Children's. Johnny's sleeping and doing okay.>

ALSO BY KARY JANE HUTTO

The Trouble With Blondie

www.ingramcontent.com/pod-product-compliance
Lightning Source LLC
Chambersburg PA
CBHW060624310726
48982CB00003B/668